Discarded Treasures

Twenty-five Shades of Dead

Harold Kempka

I0670946

Night to Dawn Magazine & Books LLC

ISBN: 978-1-937769-38-3
Cover Illustration by Teresa Tunaley
Editor: Barbara Custer
All rights reserved.

Night to Dawn Magazine & Books LLC
P. O. Box 643
Abington, PA 19001
www.bloodredshadow.com

Table of Contents

Introduction

Welcome to "Discarded Treasures," twenty five short tales of skin-crawling, leave-the-lights-on prose. Do you remember the scary stories told around a campfire and how everyone scoffed at and dismissed as not being real? Why was it that no one wanted to take the path to the showers or bathroom alone?

You knew there were no monsters in the woods stalking young campers, so what caused the snapping twigs and rustling bushes you just heard? Nearly everyone at one time or another will experience the discomfort of being alone in a darkened bedroom, especially in one you are unfamiliar with. After all, who knows what lurks in the shadows?

The stories herein will rekindle those childhood fears you thought you outgrew. *Discarded Treasures*, the anthology's namesake, tells of a bag lady rummaging through the refuse of overindulgence for discarded items other people no longer have use for. "Wild Goose Chase" brings to your door the relative you loathe and wish you did not have.

The great winter storms of 2015 wreaked havoc across the country. One woman in "When the Ice Man Cometh" discovers that when she ventures out on a short jaunt to the store to replenish supplies.

Women since the beginning of time have hated their monthly curse, and in "The Curse" you get an idea why. In "The Reflection," a woman discovers a vanity in the attic of a newly bought home

Earth consciousness and finding a remedy for global warming and devastation of the world's rain forests are a hot topic in my story "Reparation," where there may just be a cure on the horizon, however unpleasant it may seem.

"Trick or Treat" tells of a holiday gone wrong, while other stories reveal a date night that may not meet your expectations, and a hike through the woods that brings a strange discovery. Not to be outdone, in "Naughty and Nice," a man walking home from work on Christmas eve wallows in his Scrooge-like disdain for the holiday season.

Believe me, there is hell to be raised in these pages, as in "Homecoming" when an unexpected houseguest arrives, or of discovering that vampires make for lousy dates no matter how refined or well-dressed they are as is the case in "Pest Control."

Travelers occasionally discover as in "No Rest for the Weary," the only vacancy to be found is at a motel that should be condemned, or they stop in a town named "Redemption" where everyone is welcome and sin is forgiven.

My story "Winner" shows how first job interviews are always stressful, and that the promise of employment with a powerhouse company may result in unexpected fringe benefits.

However, some of you will still not admit your heart rate sometimes spikes when you hear that bump in the night or scratching on the wall while you are reading or trying to fall asleep. Was it just the wind or is there an intruder, waiting to violate you when you are most vulnerable?

Who among you has never gone to bed without experiencing a brief second of terror upon feeling a slight movement in the mattress, as though something may be crawling beneath it, or feel a tug at the covers from the other side of the bed when you sleeping alone. Do you convince yourself it was all in your mind and drift off to sleep or do you lie awake and wonder?

At one time or another in our lives, our own discarded little treasures, be they objects, places, people, or memories relegated to the dusty corridors in our minds, will rise from the depths. They will torment us about what could have been or something that never should have been said or done. In closing, think happy thoughts my friends. I hope your treasures, material or otherwise that you have collected and discarded, don't turn on you.

Happy reading,
Hal Kempka

Discarded Treasures

Violet dug through the alley dumpster sitting behind a gutted apartment building. After removing a lamp, battered toaster, and a few other discarded treasures, as she called them, she set them in her shopping cart between bulging plastic bags of recyclables.

She pushed the cart through the murky depths of the downtown alley and stepped onto the street. The putrid stench of grime and urine from her soiled clothing preceded her. Passersby scurried past in a wide arc around her.

A muffled cry emerged from a bassinet strapped to the cart's child seat. Several people walking past stopped and craned their necks with concerned stares. Violet ignored them and continued down the street, mumbling something unintelligible into the bassinet.

Several blocks later, a police squad car pulled up to the curb beside her. The officer stepped from the car and motioned her to him.

"Good afternoon Ma'am. We received a call a while ago about a baby crying."

He nodded toward the basket and asked, "May I take a look?"

Violet flashed the officer a toothless grin. "Officer, do I look like I should have me a damned baby in here?"

"Well, I'm just responding to a citizen's complaint."

She gave a rasping, hacking cough and then spit on the street. "Well then here, take a look."

She grumbled under her breath and pulled back a tattered and gritty baby blanket covering the bassinet. The officer leaned forward but jumped back, gasping.

Violet cackled and slapped her knee. She pulled the blanket back farther, giving the officer a better view. A relieved look flooded his face as he stared down at an antique doll with oxidized, porcelain arms. The doll mechanically raised and lowered its arms and looked the same size as a baby.

Spider web cracks covered the porcelain, which felt cold when he touched it. At the same time, the doll's dull marbled eyes fluttered open and shut. The officer stepped away from the bassinet and cart when a bug crawled from a small hammerhead-sized hole marring the side of its brittle, cracked face.

"Now, does this look like some damn baby to you, officer?" Violet asked.

"To be honest, ma'am, if I had only seen it from a distance, I would have thought it was."

He questioned her for several more

minutes and then drove off. She muttered several obscenities and turned to the doll.

"Oooh, my little prince, did that mean man scare you?"

Violet shook the baby doll's chest and it echoed a scratchy, "Mama, Mama."

She chuckled and leaned into the bassinet whispering, "Well, I know you are getting hungry. But have patience, and old Violet will get us some dinner."

After kissing its forehead, she covered it once again with the blanket. Violet continued down the sidewalk muttering and laughing. She waited out of sight behind a delicatessen as the evening shadows cast a pall over the alley.

Shortly after closing, the deli clerks threw several boxes of leftovers and outdated food into the dumpster. After they left, Violet dug through the garbage and batted away several rats trying to grab the food from her hands.

One scampered out of the dumpster and disappeared into her grocery cart. She could hear it digging through the rancid garbage piled around the bassinet.

"Go find your own food, you damned hairballs!" Violet yelled.

She swung a cut-off broom handle against the cart's steel basket. The rat scurried out of the cart and disappeared into the alley shadows. She dropped a few more items into the cart, before pushing it down the maze of dank-smelling alleys.

"Well, my little prince," she said patting the blanket, "I would say we had a good night."

Upon reaching a dumpster pushed against the alcove of an old abandoned building, she moved it enough to slide between the dumpster and building with her cart. Once she pulled the dumpster back in place, she opened a small door and pushed the cart inside.

Violet slid a thick wooden beam across the doorway to keep out unwanted visitors. After lighting several candles, she sat on a dirty, torn couch and munched on a moldy clump of roast beef.

The cart rustled and she caught a glimpse of a rat digging through her treasures.

"Get out of there, you damn freeloader!" She yelled and kicked the cart with her foot. The rat surfaced through the garbage and scampered out of sight.

Violet stood and shuffled over to the cart. Her cackle echoed across the candlelit room as she peered into the bassinet. The doll clutched the rat between its hands and busily tore away fur and flesh. Violet patted the doll's belly.

"Now, didn't I tell you we would be eating soon? You can always trust old Violet, my baby."

The doll's bloodied lips curled into a smile. Between bites it cooed, "Mama!"

Ophelia

Ophelia lay naked on a stainless steel gurney in the county morgue. Two days earlier, the police discovered her bloated and battered body on her apartment floor, beaten to death by a jealous wife. The reeking stench of decomposition filled the sun-warmed apartment.

A hungry, plague-infected rat slipped into the morgue. It skittered across the cold cement floor and climbed the gurney. The odor of disinfectant hung heavy in the air as it crawled alongside the chilled corpse beneath the sterile sheet. Upon reaching her skull, the rat gnawed through the soft tissue and into the inner ear canal.

Rapidly spreading plague cells immediately began fermenting the decomposing tissue. Inside Ophelia, neurons began firing like sparkplugs as if trying to jumpstart the lifeless corpse.

An assistant coroner stepped into the room and spotted the rat cradling a segment of Ophelia's tissue between its paws. He tiptoed across the room with a mallet raised over his head. The rat splattered against the stainless steel gurney like a tomato.

Six months after the funeral, Ophelia suddenly awakened in dank darkness. Her milky, opaque eyes provided her with a night vision of sorts, and she could see the shadowy interior of her casket. She also felt an awareness of its soft, silky padding.

The casket, having cracked beneath the weight of the earth, allowed in worms and bugs that had begun to feed on her. Although this was now her eternal home, a primal urge for flesh and brain matter commanded her to rise to the surface periodically and feed as well. The broken record repetition stirred her body into action.

Ophelia's calcified fingernails clawed at the wooden casket until she ripped through. She dug upward through the musty earth, spitting mouthfuls of dirt. Her hand broke the surface, scattering clods of sod about the plot while she clawed at the sky.

The other arm followed and she pulled herself from her grave. She stood and faltered on legs no longer equipped with muscle tone. Although she had no conscious awareness of what transpired, the virus transmitted the commands she needed to follow.

Her body clock regulated her every action, including the need to feed only in darkness. She had a narrow window of opportunity for flesh. The grassy ground beneath her took on a flat, freshly mown appearance; it would revert to an open state for her return once she climbed back into her casket.

Fleeting thoughts of her former life registered occasionally like electrical jolts. Ophelia caught a glimpse of how she had once delighted in driving men out of their minds. It seemed that even after joining the undead her subconscious still registered her desire for men. The difference now was inflicting pain rather than pleasure as she sucked their life from them.

She stumbled toward town, keeping to the shadows in the alleyway adjacent to the busy boulevard. Her stained, tattered gown billowed behind her in the breeze.

Transients crawling from cubbyholes and cardboard shelters to begin their nightly foraging spotted her. As Ophelia passed by, she bared her rotting teeth and snarled. They immediately retreated to the safety of their shelters.

She stood in a dark and damp alcove and waited. Finally, a young couple wandered out of a night club and walked several yards down the alley. They leaned against the cold brick building, kissing and embracing.

Ophelia stepped from the shadows and flicked her hand at the young man. With one swipe, her jagged fingernails ripped his throat out. The girl opened her mouth to scream, but Ophelia's other hand reached out and crushed her throat.

After pulling her to the ground, she tore into the girl's sweet, tender belly flesh. The sickly sweet steam from the freshly exposed viscera rose into the cool evening. After she consumed her fill, Ophelia's ecstatic snarl echoed down the alley.

She retraced her steps to the cemetery, leaving the two disfigured corpses as carrion for feral creatures that hunted the city alleyways. Once a robber of men's hearts, Ophelia had become a robber of flesh and brains; she was here to stay.

Long Live the Queen

Edward's lanky frame allowed him room to easily follow the narrow walkway between the walls of the reptile and insect exhibits. While he dropped a scoop of crickets into each terrarium, he occasionally peered through the glass, getting a creature's eye view of the crowd.

He loved his new job as a janitor. Even though he earned just above minimum wage, the curator gave him the job of feeder when the new insect and reptile exhibit opened. To help out, he arranged tuition free classes at the local college for Edward.

The new exhibit drew a larger than expected crowd and the steady stream of people seemed unending. As he neared the end of the row Edward's ex-girlfriend Sheila, strolled past arm in arm with some guy he'd never seen before.

Sheila broke his heart two years earlier, and he thought he'd gotten over her. His stomach churned though, seeing her with another guy. Perhaps now that he had a job, she might consider getting back together. When they walked past the door, he stepped out.

"Hello Sheila," he said, tapping her on the shoulder.

She turned, startled. "Oh Edward! What are you doing here?"

"Sorry. I was feeding the reptiles and saw you through the glass. I just wanted to say, hi."

"Oh, okay," she said. "How long have you been here?"

"About six months."

She introduced her friend and he told her he would meet her at the exhibit exit and left.

After he'd gone, Edward said, "I tried calling several times, though I guess you were out."

"Actually, I was home," she replied. "I have caller ID, remember?"

"Then, why didn't you answer?"

"I had nothing to say. You were jobless and couldn't support me the way I thought a man should."

"But things change," Edward replied. "I can take care of you now."

"Edward, stop with the fairy tales. You're a janitor."

"I clean the exhibits and feed the creatures, too. I'm also the night watchman and attend classes. They're giving me a research position after I graduate."

"That's great," she said. "Listen, I have to go meet my friend."

"Do you want to get together sometime? You know, get a cup of coffee or something. How about tonight after the museum closes? I'll let you in the back, we'll order out for dinner and talk as friends."

"I don't know, Edward. Maybe, if I don't have plans."

****

After the museum closed, Edward stepped into a large glass enclosure containing native South American plants and insects. He followed a stone path through the flora and a praying mantis as big as his hand hopped onto his shoulder.

After feeding it a cricket, Edward dropped several handfuls onto the carpet of leaves and twigs. He hurried to the exit as two black waves of thumb-sized, pincher-wielding army ants crawled from under the leaves. Their pinchers clicked while they satisfied their voracious appetite.

Upon returning to his office, Edward spotted a small package on the desk addressed to him. The enclosed jar inside contained a bulbous black and brown army ant queen. An attached note from the museum director instructed him to carefully place it in the colony's exhibit.

He stayed in his office and ordered out for a pizza, hoping Sheila would return. He needed to prove how special she was to him. When an hour passed and Sheila didn't show, he grabbed the jar and started for the exhibit.

The metal service doors banged several times. He jumped and nearly dropped the jar.

"Hold on!"

Sheila stood with her hands on her hips, frowning when he opened the door.

"Did you forget I might come by?"

"No, I just thought you weren't going to show."

"Well, I'm here, but don't get your hopes up."

He led her back to the tiny office. Sheila gazed at the ant through the jar and tapped the glass.

"So this is your big project, huh?"

"Part of it," he said. "Come on, I have to place it with the colony."

When he unlocked the glass enclosure, Edward stepped through the door. He motioned to Sheila to step in with him. She stood frozen in place however, cringing at the oversized mantises, finger-thick walking sticks, and turtle-sized black beetles crawling all over.

"No way!" she cried.

"Come on, these are all harmless. The army ants are harmless as well, unless they are disturbed. As soon as I put the queen with the colony we'll leave. The queen lives out her life being waited on and I would wait on you if you were my queen."

She rolled her eyes and stepped inside the enclosure. Edward removed the lid and handed Sheila the jar.

"Here, hold this a moment while I locate the colony."

She stood at the edge of the walkway while he lifted leaves and logs looking for the colony. When she spotted a large violet orchid, Sheila stepped toward the foliage to get a closer look.

Edward spun around when her frantic screams broke the silence. She was kicking her legs and batting at a thick swath of black ants that had crawled up past her knees.

As he started toward her, she stumbled backward and tripped. Sheila fell to the floor and the queen fell from the jar onto her chest. The large ants hurried toward their queen, and covered Sheila from head to toe. They bit and tore at her swelling flesh while she writhed about on the leafy carpet, screaming in agony.

A column of agitated ants started toward Edward. He hurried from the enclosure and watched, horrified yet oddly intrigued by the colony's efficiency as they stripped away her flesh.

Shortly before dawn Edward returned to the enclosure with a large trash bag for Sheila's bony remains. He took them home and disposed of them through the wood chipper in his garage. He would find a woman to be his queen and until then, he'd found a solution on dealing with those rejecting him.

Atonement

The vacant, burned out cathedral stood on the street corner like a tombstone announcing the death of the city's lower east side. Artie found a broken basement window in the rear of the church. He scrambled inside to escape the February evening's bitter wind.

A fire gutted the church months earlier, leaving it empty until the parish could demolish and rebuild it. But even with insurance, hard economic times postponed their plans. The homeless and rail yard transients like Artie occasionally laid claim to the vacant building, though neighbors' complaints to the police resulted in regular crackdowns and evictions.

As he climbed the stairs to the gutted sanctuary, the aroma of melting candle wax hung in the air. He noticed several lit candles lining the half-destroyed, ash-stained alter. *Who the hell else was here,* he wondered.

Artie stayed in the darkness of the sanctuary's side aisle. He spotted a graffiti-covered confessional that sat in a darkened corner of the church. He hurried to it and slipped through the narrow door. The odor of urine and soiled clothing gagged him.

While it stunk, at least he could get a good night's sleep. He peered through the heavy mesh screen dividing the polished oak cubicle, wondering about all the sins privately revealed there over the years.

The confessional door on the opposite side of the screen opened and Artie leaned back into the darkness. He pulled a switchblade from his pocket as a shadowy figure stepped inside and removed a small candle from a large briefcase.

A match flared long enough to light it, and Artie recognized a priest's smock and clerical collar square.

He left the knife unfolded but slid it into his pocket. The priest whispered a short prayer and crossed himself.

"Have you come to confess your sins, my son?" he asked, catching Artie off guard.

"H-how did you know I was here, Father?" Artie asked from the darkened cubicle.

"I saw you enter the sanctuary. I sometimes come here to offer salvation to wayward souls such as you."

"Well, you're lucky you're a priest," Artie said. "I might have hurt you."

"How's that?"

The candlelight reflected off the switchblade, which Artie waved across the screen.

"I thought you were some goombah invading my turf."

"Sounds like you need to seek absolution."

"Nah," Artie replied. "I just want to spend a night out of the cold."

"I see," the priest replied, sounding disappointed.

"But, you know what, Father?" Artie said. "As long as we are here, let's do this confession thing."

"Bless you, my son. When I leave, I'll make sure no one knows you were even here. And by the way, don't worry about the police. They don't come around anymore."

"All righty then," Artie said. "Forgive me, Father, for I have sinned. I haven't been to confession in many years."

After several silent seconds, the priest asked, "Is that all you have to confess?"

"Well Father, I haven't exactly lived the life of an altar boy. But, if I confessed everything, we'd be here for a month."

"I have all the time in the world. Receiving absolution requires you to confess your sins, regardless of their significance."

"But what if it's a felony, like rape or murder? Won't you have to report it to the police?"

"No. Your confession is between you and God. I'm only the facilitator."

Artie rambled on about petty crimes, like shoplifting and stiffing restaurants for a meal.

Finally, the priest said, "Look, isn't there some serious sin you have to confess?"

"Well, Father, once in the park across town I mugged and killed a guy. Another time, I stole a car and robbed the First Federal bank; shot the guard on that one, but he lived. The cops never found out who did either of them jobs."

"So," the priest said, "you've lived your life by dealing with the devil, and now you want God's forgiveness."

"Yeah, something like that," Artie said. "How about it, Father? Am I forgiven?"

"It's not that simple. You need to turn yourself in to the police."

"But I don't want to go to jail," Artie replied. "I just want you to forgive my sins."

"The wages of sin are proportionate to your crime, and it will require the harshest of penance. Are you ready to accept that?"

"Anything," Artie said. "I just want absolution."

"When is the last time you received Communion?"

"It's been so long I can't remember."

"Then, follow me!"

"Whoa, hold on! Where are we going?"

"You need to first receive Communion, and then your penance."

"Isn't it usually the other way around?" Artie asked.

"Yes, but your sins must be dealt with differently."

Artie followed him, figuring he'd at least get a free drink out of it. He knelt on the altar steps while the priest removed altar sacraments from the briefcase. He fed Artie a wafer and poured a small goblet of dark wine.

"Drink all of it, my son."

Artie remembered Communion glasses being more like thimbles. But he drank the goblet's contents. Its bitter aftertaste reminded him how lousy sacramental wine tasted.

Rather than bless him, the priest said, "Now, you shall receive your atonement."

Artie stood. The room began spinning and he passed out. When he regained consciousness, he realized he'd been bound and gagged. He was also lying naked on the cold, marble alter.

The priest stood before him. In the candlelight, his black eyes smoldered from deep in their sockets. A rubber apron replaced the collar and smock.

"Forgive me, Father, but I have sinned," the priest said. He burst into laughter and continued, "Guys like you are a hoot!"

His face radiated with a crazed grin as he reached into the briefcase.

"You are hereby absolved of your sins. Go in peace."

Duct tape muffled Artie's screams and he could only gaze in a horrified stupor at the large meat cleaver swinging toward him in a swift, fluid arc.

A Wild Goose Chase

Upon arriving home from school, Benny's mom hollered from the kitchen, "Benny, your Uncle George has come to visit!"

Benny rolled his eyes and walked into the kitchen. "Hey, Uncle George. What's up?"

He hated it when his uncle came to visit. He was a mean slob that loved to terrorize Benny, or pinch and pick on him whenever his mom wasn't looking.

George slouched against the kitchen chair with his shirt unbuttoned from the ribcage down. His ample, hairy belly buried the belt and buckle holding up his worn, shiny pants. In all, Uncle George was the same smelly, slovenly blob he always had been.

Upon spotting Benny, George jumped to his feet and playfully grabbed his slightly built nephew in a headlock.

"Well, if it isn't my favorite nephew! Damn, you ain't much bigger than the last time I visited."

The washing machine buzzer sounded, and Benny's mom started toward the laundry room.

"You boys talk for a bit while I put that load in the dryer."

As soon as she left the room, George rubbed his meaty knuckles against the top of the boy's bushy, russet-haired head. Then, he pushed him away. Benny hated the way his uncle always bullied him.

"So, what have you been doing for fun, 'ya little dork? Playing with dolls?"

"Ha-ha very funny," Benny replied. "I have been exploring down by the creek."

George smirked. "Oh, whooptey doo! There isn't anything down there except some skunks, rabbits, and snakes."

Benny's eyes lit up. "But Uncle George, there is! I discovered a monster down by the creek that eats people."

"There's no monster down there, ya little pipsqueak." George said.

"Yes, there is."

"No there isn't. You're just going on a wild goose chase."

"Well, I'm going down to find it tomorrow. You can come with me unless you're chicken."

Benny tucked his hands into his armpits and walked around the kitchen clucking. George grabbed his nephew by the throat and pulled him close.

"Listen, you punk, if you ever call me a chicken again, I'll rip you apart myself. Got that?"

""S-sure, Uncle," Benny rasped, trying to pry his uncle's fingers free. "Sorry."

His uncle thought for a second, and his lips curled in a wry smile. "You know, maybe I will go with you."

George scraped his claw-like, beefy fingers down his nephew's chest and continued, "And if there is one, I might just let it catch you, and watch while it tears your arms and legs off. You remember what happened to the bratty Hawkins kid, don't you? The one you said bullied you around a few years ago."

"Stop it, George!" Benny's mom hollered, stepping back into the room. "Don't scare him by bringing all that up again. You know the papers said it was a mountain lion that came down from the hills."

"Yeah, well," her brother said, "he brought up the monster thing to begin with. Besides, maybe that's what the papers wanted you to believe."

After breakfast the next morning, Benny and his uncle stopped by the garage. George smirked and suggested they bring some weapons, just in case. He found a couple of ax handles, and gave one to Benny.

They hiked through the woods making no effort to be quiet and trampled through the thickets of wild raspberries and undergrowth. A hundred yards ahead, Benny heard the creek bubbling over the rocks.

"We're almost there, Uncle George," he said in a deliberate whisper.

Upon reaching the creek bank, his uncle pointed toward the water. "Okay, Bennie, you walk that way and check along the creek.

I'll go up into the woods. If there is one, I'll scare it down to you. Now, make sure you watch for him, cause if you don't, he's gonna get you."

"O-o-k-a-y, Uncle," Bennie said. "But not if he gets you first."

"You little smart ass," Uncle George grumbled. "You're gonna get yours."

After a half hour of walking back and forth along the creek, Bennie heard loud rustling in the thickets up the hill. He squatted behind a bush to watch. His Uncle George crashed through the thickets, his face ashen and his eyes the size of silver dollars.

He waved his arms like a wild man and Benny noticed that the brambles had bloodied them and torn his clothes.

George ran past his nephew screaming, "Aaah! Aaah! Get out of here, Benny. The monster's coming."

He leapt into the creek and Benny fought back a giggle. Then, a hulking, two-legged creature, covered in course brown hair with a pug nose and gnarled ears bounded through the brush. It jumped the creek bank and landed on George. Benny listened to his uncle's screams amid the loud grunting and splashing.

While he watched from the bushes, a faint smile crossed Benny's lips. The creek ran red with blood as the creature ripped his uncle apart with its long, serrated teeth.

The creature stopped and sniffed the air with its pug nose. Whipping its head around, it glared at Benny. The boy nodded and seconds later, the creature bounded up the opposite bank and into the woods, carrying Uncle George's lifeless body between its large jowls.

Benny took his time returning home, knowing he made good on his promise to occasionally feed the creature. He reported his uncle missing to the police and after a thorough search, they found no trace of George, except for one shoe with a large bite out of the heel.

****

The next fall when Benny entered junior high school, Eddie Bogan, the class bully, shoved him against the lockers after gym class.

"Give me all your lunch money, kid, or I'll beat you to a pulp."

"Okay." Benny reached into his pocket.

Before handing Eddie three crumpled up dollar bills, he continued, "Say, you know what? I'll bet you my lunch money every day for the rest of the year that you don't have the guts to go with me into the woods by the river and see a real monster."

"You calling me a chicken? I'll bust up your face, punk."

"If you come with me, I'll prove it. If there isn't one, you can smash my face and take my lunch money."

"You better not be messin' with me, man," the boy said. "I'll meet you there after school."

That afternoon, Benny met Eddie and they stepped into the trees. As they trudged toward the creek banging sticks together and shouting, Benny smiled. All he needed to do now was go to the creek and have Eddie scare the monster through the trees toward him.

Housewarming

Two weeks after buying the dilapidated Victorian, Levon moved in. His great-grandparents had built it at the turn of the century, only to lose it during the Great Depression. The state converted it into a home for unwed mothers, but shut it down after a series of questionable adoptions and the mysterious disappearance of several young mothers.

Since then, it had been repeatedly occupied and abandoned. When the state put it up for auction, Levon saw an opportunity to bring it back into the family. He would refurbish it to its original splendor.

After submitting the winning bid, he decided that converting it into a bed and breakfast would prove more profitable.

He spent most of move-in day, directing which boxes belonged in the different rooms. The musty odor of old, heavily waxed oak floors and moldings lent a hypnotic ambiance he hoped his future guests would appreciate and remember.

While taking a break that afternoon, Levon found an old desk covered by a sheet shoved to the rear of the parlor closet. He inadvertently pulled a drawer out too far and discovered a key that had fallen behind it. He tried various doors, from the cellar to the upstairs bedrooms, but the key didn't fit.

He opened a narrow door at the end of the hall thinking it was a closet. It had no lock and opened to a stairwell that led to the attic. While the old rusting key unlocked the attic door, the wood had swelled against the jamb and it was stuck shut.

Levon slammed his shoulder against it until it flew open. A rush of chilling and sickly, foul-smelling air escaped.

He stepped into the room and swept the flashlight beam across it. A transom on the far wall offered more light. When he opened the louvers, fresh air rushed in and bright white shafts of dusty sunlight sprayed the room.

Large faded splotches splattered the warped, dust-laden wood floor and walls. He explored the attic and rummaged through several old mattresses and bed frames as well as faded furniture and broken chairs, wondering what could be refurnished.

A stack of dusty, cobwebbed boxes sat stacked in a dark corner. Most contained moth-eaten clothes that needed to be disposed of. He found a wooden box shoved to the back and unlatched it. A putrid wispy odor escaped its confines and dissipated. Inside the box, he found a couple of teddy bears, baby clothes, and booties, and a wrinkled, faded photo of a young woman holding a tiny baby.

Although she smiled into the camera, her eyes suggested anything but happiness. Levon spotted a newspaper clipping in the bottom of the box. The young woman disappeared after losing her baby. A county-wide search proved unsuccessful though the case culminated in the state permanently shutting down the home.

The afternoon sunlight through the transom began to fade and Levon decided he ought to get a little more unpacking done. Once he settled in, he would come back up. The room had potential to become a honeymoon suite with a large window for light and all the amenities a newlywed couple might desire.

****

He awakened shortly after midnight to noises downstairs. They sounded as though someone was rummaging through the kitchen cupboards. Levon slipped out of bed and grabbed his four-iron from the golf bag leaning against the wall.

He tiptoed to the landing and peeked through the banister slats. The moonlight shining through the Victorian's window cast the downstairs in a silvery patina.

A shadow moved across the light, and Levon pressed his back against the wall. He sidestepped down the stairs at a slow steady pace. Upon reaching the bottom of the stairs, he crept across the room through the maze of haphazardly placed furniture and boxes.

Levon edged up to the kitchen door and peeked around the corner.

A woman with long, stringy hair hanging over her shoulders rummaged through the cupboards. She made no attempt to be quiet. Moonlight shining through the kitchen window outlined her bone-thin, soiled body through her diaphanous, tattered nightgown.

Levon stared transfixed as she removed a bottle from the cleaning cupboard. After unscrewing it, she held it to her nose. Wild, milky eyes floated in the dark shadows of her sockets. Strips of pasty flesh hung from her decaying, once youthful face.

"I'll fix you all for stealing my baby, you bastards," she rasped.

She lifted the bottle to her lips. Bugs crawled freely in and out of her facial orifices as she let out a hoarse cackle and gulped it down. Smoke swirled out of her mouth while the Drano burned her throat.

Levon gagged on the odor and the woman swung around, hissing and snarling.

Levon poised his golf club as though about to tee off.

"Wh-who are you and what do you want?"

The waiflike woman said nothing and rose off the floor. She leapt through the air and knocked him to the floor with unbelievable strength. As Levon lay stunned, she dropped to the floor and straddled him.

Her powerful legs pinned his arms to his side and she lowered her head toward his.

She lapped at his face with a blackened, rotting tongue, leaving a trail of putrid slobber. Her putrid breath felt hot against his skin.

"All that matters is, you are a man," she replied, in a gravelly whisper. "Your kind done it to me and the other girls that lived here; but you took them from us. Now you're going to do it to me and let me keep it."

"Do what?" Levon cried, twisting like a madman trying to free himself from her grip. "I don't know what you are talking about!"

"You're going to love me and give me my baby!"

She feverishly kissed and licked him all over. A drop of what felt like a sticky tear slid off her cheek.

The vengeful wraith began to move her body against his. She began slowly and built up to a violent frenzy that chafed him. Levon could only fix his terror-filled eyes on the ceiling and fight the urge to respond. She continued until he relented.

Without warning, she let out a shrill scream that echoed through the room. The wraith sunk her teeth into his neck. Blood gushed in spurts as she ripped away the flesh.

"This is MY house now!" she squealed, hovering over Levon's jerking, twitching corpse. "You will always love me and our baby shall live forever."

Eyes of the Beholder

Dirk searched the Village Green part of town, and finally found the Art Cosmos gallery. The flyer he'd found on a coffeehouse end table was promoting a new artist's work. It described the gallery as a place for those drawn to the avant-garde and unusual.

The gallery sat off the main drag in a darkened alley, with a single 60-watt light bulb illuminating the sign over the door.

When he stepped inside, the throng of guests interrupted their conversations long enough to cast a quick stare at the new arrival. Well dressed and coiffed trendsetters clinked champagne glasses with jack-booted Goths whose piercings, tattoos, gaudy makeup and somber attire seemed more appropriate for an anarchy march rather than an art showing.

Felicia, the drag queen owner, greeted him like he was an old friend with a quick hug and an air kiss on the cheek.

"Welcome to my gallery, you handsome devil. I've not seen you here before, so please sign my guestbook, sweetie. I do want to know who you are."

A waiter handed each of them a flute of champagne. After chatting a moment, Felicia excused himself and strode off to flit amongst the crowd. Dirk followed the critics and patrons through a series of ceiling-lit paintings hung on maze-like room dividers.

They stopped and studied each painting, entranced by the ostensible interaction of surreal relief and sculpture. The crimson signature canted in the lower right corner read simply, Carmella.

Several patrons referred to her collection as exquisite, entrancing, bizarre, chilling, and frighteningly attractive. Dirk thought it more attuned to chilling and bizarre.

"Do you like my work?"

The deep, sultry voice in the shadows startled him. Dirk spun around, spilling wine on his jacket. A sultry, gaunt-faced woman lingered on the fringe of the darkened corner.

"Oh! I didn't see you standing there," he said, dabbing the spill on his lapel with a napkin. "And to answer your question, yes, I do like your work. It is quite out of the ordinary."

She brushed a shock of auburn hair from her face. "I didn't mean to startle you. I'm Carmella, the so-called honored artist. And thank you, I think, for that compliment."

Her dilated, apple green eyes burned through him in an intense stare. Dirk's initial reaction was that she was an odd duck. However, he felt a strange though uneasy attraction toward her.

She said it was her first professional showing, and Felicia billed it as Carmella's "coming out" party.

Her discomfort about being in the limelight had kept her standing in the shadows most of the evening. She feared that Felicia's patrons would deem her work amateurish and not appreciate the passion she put into each piece. Watching from the shadows and listening to their comments took some of the edge off.

"Well, you sound starved," Dirk said, as her stomach emitted a hungry growl. "Can I get you some hors d'oeuvres?"

He returned with a small plate of cheese and crackers, and she led him from painting to painting. Each one represented something of the human condition, she explained. She used the papier-mâché body parts and household implements to convey that people were expendable resources, no different than the everyday trash they discarded.

While her work both attracted and repulsed the patrons, Dirk noticed "sold" tags taped to several.

They stopped and stood before an eight by ten foot painting titled "Blame." Arrows aimed at the outstretched index finger of an acrylic hand that pointed outward at the viewer. Carmella squeezed his arm and gave a quiet chuckle when a visitor standing in a finger's line of sight, shivered and stepped aside.

In her piece "The Big Bang," swirling kaleidoscopic colors exploded across the canvas from various sized pistols. Deep red blotches of crimson enamel ran down the canvas from the bas-reliefs of shattered, textured faces.

"Blinded Visions," however, drew the largest crowd. Broken eyeglasses and florescent eyeballs filled the black light-illuminated, midnight blue canvas. Silvery tears dripped from a single pair of bright blue eyes that were placed on the canvas so that they could stare directly at the observer.

"My God," a woman whispered as they walked past. "I can't imagine what the artist was thinking, but this is brilliant."

Carmella glanced at Dirk, barely able to contain her smile. As the showing came to a close, Felicia introduced Carmella to the gallery crowd. Her timid stance broadened and her head rose erect when cheers and applause filled the room.

Well-wishers and hangers-on swarmed her, and after a few minutes, Dirk noticed her beginning to hyperventilate. He seized the opportunity and dragged her away from the crowd.

Walking her to her car, Dirk said, "Carmella, I am very attracted to you and would like to see you again."

She pressed against him and gave him a peck on the cheek. "Then, why don't you follow me home and we can get to know each other better."

A half hour out of town, Carmella turned onto a long dirt drive. Upon arriving at a secluded cabin, Dirk stepped from the car. He breathed in the refreshing Balsam scent permeating the night air as she led him past the house.

They reached a large, rustic shed she used as her studio whenever she worked on a new project.

"Don't you ever find the seclusion occasionally daunting?" he asked.

"Sometimes," she said, and disappeared into another room laughing.

Moments later, Carmella returned, carrying two glasses of wine. They toasted to her success and sat on a couch. She snuggled against him and rested her head against his chest.

"Your heartbeat is so strong," she said, "It sounds like it could beat forever."

Moments later, however, Dirk's breathing turned labored and his vision blurred. As he drifted in and out of consciousness, Carmella rolled a splattered paint canvas across the floor.

She stroked his pale cheek and dragged him from the couch to the canvas. Something burned deep in Dirk's chest. He struggled to open his eyes and get to his feet, only to discover he was paralyzed and unable to move. He could not feel his body involuntarily twitch while she drew a scalpel down his chest and over his belly.

The following morning, Carmella hurried to her studio and assembled her new supply of materials. After making several corrections to her sketch, she retrieved the gurney from the walk-in freezer containing Dirk's cold, partially dissected corpse.

She retrieved his already papier-mâché-wrapped heart from his chest cavity and dipped them in acrylic resin. Carmella centered them on the canvas among several similar hearts. After placing his resin-coated eyes between the left and right aortas, she stood back to admire her new piece entitled, "Love at First Sight." She signed her name at the bottom in Dirk's blood.

A Quiet Lullaby

While wandering through the park on an early evening walk, Jeremy caught the faint melody of a lullaby. Thick clusters of lilac bushes lining the walkway cast twilight shadows across the path. He approached a woman sitting on a bench ahead. She bowed her head and sang to a baby bundle cradled in her arms.

"Hello," he said. "Nice evening, isn't it?"

She held the bundle against her bosom and nodded. She neither returned his gaze nor replied, however. A cold draft wafted past, sending a shiver climbing down his back.

In the lengthening shadows Jeremy distinguished nothing other than her matted disheveled hair and sallow, sunken cheeks. From her tattered and soiled clothing he surmised she might be a homeless mother from the mission several blocks away.

He continued on and lost sight of her when he rounded a bend in the path. Upon reaching the far side of the park, Jeremy turned to retrace the walk back.

A muffled growl from the bushes startled him as he rounded a bend in the path.

The hair on the back of Jeremy's neck bristled, and he looked for something to defend himself with.

He spotted a broken branch and after breaking off the stems, gripped the stick tight, ready to swing. A pair of iridescent eyes stared out at him from the shadows.

"Get out of here!" he yelled.

Jeremy broadened his shoulders in an attempt to appear larger. He prayed his aggressive tone of voice would scare whatever it was off.

When the stare continued and Jeremy saw no movement, he rustled the branches with the stick. The eyes disappeared, and when he heard movement in the bushes, he broke into a run toward the woman and child. If whatever it was harmed her or the child, he would never forgive himself.

"Miss!" he hollered, running toward them. "There is a vicious sounding animal running loose in the park. I think you ought to leave!"

The woman continued to sit on the bench and silently stare at him. He heard the growl again, this time from directly behind him. Jeremy spun and swung the stick with both hands.

It sliced through a filmy wraithlike shadow leaping at him. In mid-jump it took on a shape of a hideous, childlike creature. It knocked Jeremy to the ground with surprising strength. He grabbed the creature's shoulders and tried to push it away.

Its face felt cold and clammy, and the snapping jaws stretched toward him with a gruesome elasticity. Jeremy's screams dissolved into a muffled gurgle as the creature ripped out his throat.

Curved claws jutting from its small chubby fingers shredded his clothes and disemboweled him. The woman watched in wide-eyed silence with her lips curled in a slight smile.

Blood spurted in concert with his heartbeat, and a dark crimson pool formed beneath him. While the ghoulish creature feasted on the steaming viscera, it edged sideways to allow the woman to kneel beside it. Once they were sated, the mother stroked her baby's head and lifted it into her arms.

"Come, my baby. We have fed enough. It's time to go."

The ghoulish toddler's clawed hands grabbed onto her dirt-stained dress while it nestled against her. The mother hummed a quiet lullaby as they faded into a translucent vapor and wafted over the dew-covered grass. They disappeared into the indigo darkness of the cemetery across the street, to rest until their need for sustenance arose once again.

Leave a Business Card

The open house ad for an aging Victorian appeared in the city paper's real estate section. While it was a forty mile drive to the small town, a free meal was offered. Benny felt certain the local yokel wouldn't know its real value and figured it could be an easy con.

Upon reaching the town, Benny found the directions confusing. He pulled his sleek Mercedes into the town's single-pump gas station. An old man sat slouched in a chair by the door. The fedora shielding his eyes bobbed in concert with his snoring.

"Pardon me," Benny called out after lowering the window. "Do you know how to get the old Oliver place?"

The old man sat up with a start. Deep-set, tired eyes rested on cheeks of scruffy gray stubble. He peered out from beneath the brim and spit a gob of tobacco juice into a coffee can spittoon.

"Yep," he said, ignoring the russet-colored trickle sliding onto his chin.

Benny awaited a further response and getting none said, "So, old timer, how do I get there?"

The man raised a bony finger and pointed down Main Street.

"The name's Claude, and not old timer. Take the road out of town three quarters of a mile. Stay to the left when the road forks. After another mile, turn left. When you get to the four mile bridge turn left again to a gravel road. Follow it to the house."

"Thanks."

"Are you going out there for the home tour and free dinner advertised in the city papers?"

"Yeah, why?"

"Are you a serious buyer or a lookie loo wanting a free dinner? I don't think they take kindly to either."

"I'm a realtor specializing in Victorian resales. If it's in the condition advertised in the paper, I'm sure the owner will come down to what I will pay."

"Maybe and maybe not," Claude replied.

"Well, I better be on my way, Thanks for the directions."

Benny drove on through town, conjuring up scenarios he could work a scam on. Shortly after driving over the bridge, he followed Claude's directions. By the time he passed the bridge again, he realized he'd driven in one big circle.

He spotted a narrow gravel drive a few yards past the fork and grumbled, "That son of a bitch sent me on a wild goose chase."

He turned onto the gravel road and followed it. The outer condition of the three-story Victorian surprised him when he arrived. The siding looked good and the house rested on what appeared to be a solid stone foundation. A thick wooded area abutted the expanse of lush lawn.

He climbed the porch and knocked. Getting no answer, Benny peered through the leaded glass window. The heavy door creaked open several inches as he leaned against it.

He stepped into the foyer, where a cardboard sign on a small table read, *"We want to know who you are, so please leave a card for the free meal."* Benny tossed his business card on top of the others lying in a silver tray.

"Hello! Anyone here?"

A muffled voice down the hall responded, "Come in and take the stairs at the end of the hall. I'm in the basement."

Persian rug runners on the floor muffled Benny's footsteps. His heels gave a hollow echo off the wood as he crossed a gap between the rugs. The floor gave way and Benny tumbled head over heels through a trap door.

He slammed against a rack of serrated iron bars and his lungs deflated with a loud "Hunnnh!"

"Well, hello again," a voice said. "Thank you for following my directions so well. It gave me time to hurry back and greet you."

Benny's eyes swiveled toward the periphery of his vision and the vaguely familiar voice. His chest rose and fell in a shrill wheeze as he recognized Claude, the old man from the gas station. He stood next to a large brick oven. Flames licked at a chain and pulley grill hanging inside its open doors.

"I'm sorry you got the quick tour. But like I said at the gas station, son, lookie loos and real estate agents are time-wasters and just devious. Oh, I know a free meal was promised and there is for me, but not you."

The old man grabbed an axe off the woodpile. After sharpening it on a grinding wheel, he raised the axe over his head and swung. Benny lay paralyzed though his eyes widened in horror as the axe blade swung toward him.

Instead of hitting Benny, the blade swept past him and split a fire log on the floor with a loud thwack. Claude chuckled and threw it on the flames.

He raised the axe once again. Benny's horrific screams echoed only in his mind as a muffled chop coincided with the room ebbing into darkness.

Naughty and Nice

City plows scraped the streets, burying cars left on the streets and piling the heavy snow against the curbs and driveways. Felton watched helplessly from his office window as they blocked the parking lot exits, making his car inaccessible for a few days.

Of course, since it was Christmas Eve he could kiss off a ride home. Most of his employees didn't show up at all and the rest left at noon to finish last minute shopping and preparations. He continued working, hoping to set an example for his employees and was the last to leave.

He hated winter and the accompanying holiday festivities as they always caused a drop in revenue. Felton did, however, look forward to the comforting solitude of Christmas Eve, sipping a cognac by the fire and reading himself to sleep.

Felton shivered in the darkened office's morgue-like atmosphere as he shut off the lights. He buttoned his overcoat to the neck and stepped into the frigid evening for the arduous, two-mile trek home.

He trudged through ever deepening drifts, beneath a rising silver moon that cast the landscape in a glittering patina. The biting wind whipped icy crystals against Felton's face.

"Damned snow!" he grumbled, stopping to catch his breath.

A dark, billowing cloud rolled across the sky as the downtown buildings gave way to houses and apartments. The moonlight disappeared, and the streetlights' golden glow created ominous shapes in the shadows.

Wind gusts whistled in his ears, as though delivering disturbing snippets of whispered conversation like *please, let him step into the darkness.* Uneasiness gnawed at Felton's stomach and he walked faster, trying to stay under the golden aura of the street lamps.

In several hours, the darkened houses along the street would echo with laughter and squeals of excitement.

"A waste of energy and money," he grumbled out loud. To himself, he chuckled and thought, *Bah freaking humbug, you wasteful Christmas bastards.*

Parents dug themselves deeper in debt, and for what? Unappreciative children who had been taught to enjoy needless excess? One Christmas morning, those children would learn as he had the disappointment of opening meticulously wrapped presents, expecting toys and electronic gadgets only to find underwear and socks.

That experience prompted Felton's realization that Christmas and Santa were a sham and a myth. And when he found the lump of coal in his stocking, he knew it was one his father culled from the coal cellar.

"Jolly old St. Nicholas, screw you!" Felton hollered.

He'd wasted his childhood living in fear. In his young mind, Santa had been pure evil in disguise that slipped into homes down sooty chimneys to tempt nice children with toys, or terrorize them with threats that bad things happen to those who were naughty.

Felton's memories evaporated as fast as his breath in the cold night air. He heard loud scraping, and it sounded as though it came from a nearby rooftop. He scanned the roofs and then chastised himself for such childishness.

A church bell tolled midnight, and he thought, *the only place the jolly fat man lurks is in the minds of all you little brats snuggled in your beds.*

A voice growled from behind, "You should never have stopped believing, Felton."

He spun around, startled. A gaunt creature with a dark beard and leathery skin stepped from the shadows. Two hideous imps with gnarled limbs emerged from the folds of his baggy, black hooded smock.

They rushed Felton and pinned his arms to his sides in a vise-like grip. Their jagged fingernails stung as they dug into his skin. They each punched him and tore chunks of flesh from his arms and chest. Felton tried to scream, but his fear-constricted throat muscles allowed only a squeaky whisper.

The demon wrapped its withered, leathery fingers around a scythe hanging from the side of a black carriage-like hearse. The whistling blade swept through the air in a blur. Felton's severed head tumbled to the ground, saturating the fresh snow like a bright crimson snow cone.

The imps skittered back toward him. They handed the demon Felton's head before disappearing into the dark void behind the smock's thick folds. The demon carried it to the front of the carriage, where other heads impaled on rows of spikes hung like hood ornaments. He impaled Felton's dead center and climbed into the carriage.

With a crack of his whip, a team of snarling, black-tongued wolves broke into a frenzied run. As they lifted the hearse-like carriage skyward, the demon bellowed a maniacal, "Ho-ho-ho!"

The clouds cleared and moonlight once again flooded the landscape. Its silvery glow transformed the carriage into a gold-trimmed, red sleigh while the wolves grew antlers and hoofed legs. Jingling silver bells on leather straps replaced the severed heads.

The demon's beard whitened, and his face turned puffy and rosy. A pair of elves scurried from beneath his bright crimson robe into the back seat. They stuffed wrapped packages and toys into a large velvet bag for deliveries to be made to those that had been nice. Later, more coal would be left for the naughty and death given to the nonbelievers.

The Curse

The pangs of Marcie's monthly curse stabbed at her stomach. She hated that it appeared all too often without warning and never at the same time of the month. Becoming a librarian helped minimize her fear of social interaction because of its accompanying scent.

She knew what it did to her body and needed to hurry home. Basking in a hot shower would help keep the pain that accompanied it in check. After ensuring the library aisles were empty, she kicked off the black squashed heels she'd worn all day. She shoved them beneath her desk and slipped on the well-worn tennis shoes she wore to and from work.

Marcie wrapped her scarf around her head babushka-style to ward off the fall evening chill. She decided to take a shortcut through the woods and locked the doors before trotting down the steps.

She breathed in the damp air of an approaching storm as she followed the campus walkway across the commons. A crisp wind whistled through the leafless, skeletal branches of the ancient oak trees.

Marcie shivered as she walked past the few remaining buildings on the old campus toward her shortcut. The path through the woods intersected with a trail leading to one of the university's boulevards and the condominium complex where she lived.

The old buildings were slated for demolition next spring. Although she loved their gothic architecture, they were creepy. The halls of the antiquated science building still housing the anthropology department's small museum of fossil and skeletons resembled those of an abandoned asylum.

Marcie followed a worn trail into the woods. She broke into a slow run upon reaching the jogging path. Midway through the woods, a light drizzle began to fall.

The brush rustled on one side of the trail. She sensed the presence of someone else, and they were running parallel to her through the nearby underbrush. Additionally, they seemed to be matching her stride for stride.

She had run through these woods many times and knew animals larger than rabbits or squirrels were long gone. Adrenaline pumped through her veins as Marcie broke into a sprint.

Darkness fell early beneath the heavy gray cloud cover and consumed the woods. She bounded through the brush, expelling steamy clouds of breath. A lightning bolt lit up the sky followed by a deadening thunder clap.

In that brief flash of light, Marcie caught the outline of someone stopped in a clearing. They were staring at her. While she did not want a confrontation at that moment, the situation demanded it.

The resulting thunder clap resounded through the thick brush drowning out an angry growl. An anguished scream preceded the dull sound of snapping jowls, ripping flesh, and popping tendons. A deep growl rose in crescendo to a howl following several seconds of silence.

****

The storm passed before dawn. An early morning jogger notified police after discovering a muddy pair of running shoes and remains of an unidentifiable female scattered alongside the path. Yellow crime scene tape blocked off the path and disappeared in a wide circle through the woods.

Several hundred yards away, the sliding glass doors of Marcie's second floor condo balcony offered a front row view to police and medical personnel scurrying in and out of the woods. Quiet filled the condo while the post-storm, early morning sunshine warmed the room.

From beneath the covers, Marcie squinted at a sliver of light shining through the window's thick curtains. As it warmed the chill in her bedroom, she climbed out of bed. Her body ached as she stretched and hurried to the bathroom, ignoring her muddied and bloodied sheets.

Crusty bits of mud between her toes left a trail across the carpet. Marcie stepped through the shower curtain and basked in the steam-filled stall. Cloudy, rusty-brown water ran down the drain.

The hot spray soothed her skin and aching muscles, though it burned the scratches and gouges in her skin. Her hair still carried that animal smell she disliked so much, though once shampooed the sheen and fresh human aroma she loved would soon return.

After toweling off, she stood before the floor length mirror, scowling. Her mother warned her that small, fatty pockets would form along her hips and thighs as she came of age. That and her monthly curse for the hunger of human flesh would forever be the unfortunate byproduct of a werewolf's diet regimen. *That may be,* she thought, *but it does not mean I have to like or put up with it.*

Marcie walked to the patio and cast a curious gaze toward the comings and goings of police and emergency personnel. As always, they would soon come by and inquire if she might have heard or seen something.

She frowned at the blood and muddy tracks leading from the door to her bedroom. Cleaning and washing was a never ending chore, a bane no werewolf should have to endure. If only she could hire a maid she wouldn't be tempted to eat.

When the Iceman Cometh

The gentle drizzle on Monday intensified into a chilling thunderstorm by Tuesday. An arctic wind sweeping in that night plummeted temperatures to well below freezing. Television news reports warned residents to stay inside as the sudden cold snap had increased the number of deaths and missing persons.

Martha awoke the following morning shivering beneath the covers. Iced-over power lines and poles snapped, causing massive electricity blackouts. When her cell phone did not work, she figured cell towers had probably toppled beneath the weight of their icy shackles.

The sudden onslaught of ice and snow caught her off guard; her storm windows still stood in the garage, leaning against the wall. As an ominous chill whistled through narrow gaps around the windows, Martha donned her wool socks and warm-up clothes. She burrowed deeper beneath the blankets and curled into a fetal position amid its warmth. She finally forced herself to jump from bed to raise the thermostat.

Upon realizing the heater igniter would not work during an outage, she hurried toward the kitchen to put on a pot of tea. She stopped and peered through the living room's frost-covered glass. The neighborhood's ice-coated sidewalks, roofs, and buildings resembled a frozen wasteland.

Grit-blackened snowdrifts clogging the streets covered the abandoned cars. Martha tried the front door, but a sheet of frozen sleet had sealed it shut. *Damn,* she thought, *winter's Iceman had cometh with a vengeance.*

The cold wooden floor creaked beneath her feet while she hurried to the kitchen. She struck a match and lit the gas stove before filling the teapot with water. Grabbing the box of tea from the nearly empty cupboard reminded her that she needed to get to the grocery store.

Once warmed by the tea, Martha dressed and returned to the front door. She banged on it until the ice sheet broke loose, peppering the porch with jagged crystalline shards. Upon stepping outside she gasped, for the frigid air burned her lungs.

Martha retrieved an armload of firewood from the cord stacked alongside the house. After setting them beside the hearth, she grabbed her winter coat from the closet and started the two-block trek to the grocery store.

She took short, careful steps to avoid slipping on the ice hidden underneath the snow-crusted sidewalk. The neighborhood's only sign of life seemed to be several large dogs digging through a trash receptacle at Fioli's Italian restaurant. Martha noticed an unsettling wildness in their eyes when they stopped and glanced at her. Undeterred by her appearance they returned to their foraging.

Iced-over shopping carts sat scattered about the deserted parking lot at Gennaro's market when she arrived. Martha peered inside the darkened store and then turned toward home. She felt dumb for not remembering that if she had no electricity, the neighborhood market would have none as well.

A block from home, Martha spotted someone in a sooty, reddish overcoat, lugging a large, heavy looking trash bag around the corner.

"Hey there!" she called out.

The figure stopped in the shadows, and briefly stared at her before disappearing behind the house.

When she reached the dogs on the opposite side of the street, they had begun snapping at each other over a bag of garbage. They stopped and stared at her. One bared its fangs and growled.

The others joined in and she quickened her step. Upon reaching her driveway, Martha glanced over her shoulder.

The dogs had followed and now stood in the street watching her. Without warning, they scrambled after her barking and snarling as if they'd been ordered to attack. Martha rushed up the sidewalk and hurried inside.

Her heart pounded in her chest as she watched them through the window. The rib-thin dogs circled the front yard and cast hungry stares toward at her, howling repeatedly. Nausea rose in Martha's throat. Once they sniffed at the sidewalk and basement windows, the dogs turned and ran down the street.

That night, Martha curled up on the couch beneath an afghan. She sipped on a mug of brandy and tea, staring at the eerie shadows cast across the room by the flickering firelight.

She kept glancing outside, hoping the dogs would not return. When several distant explosions shook the house, Martha figured they must have come from ruptured gas mains.

When a sharp chill swept through the room, she stoked the fire and decided to spend the night on the couch. After growing drowsy from the fireplace's radiating warmth, she drifted off to sleep

A few hours later, she awakened to smoldering embers and a teeth-chattering chill. After placing more logs on the fire, she snuggled back beneath the afghan. From the corner of her eye, she caught a glimpse of a reddish image moving in the shadows.

Martha's heartrate spiked and she gasped as the man in red stepped into the flickering light. She clutched the afghan against her, gripped with fear.

"Who are you and what do you want?"

His pitch black, deep-set eyes bore through her while he walked toward the couch. Coagulated blood soaked the coat covering his large and grotesquely gnarled body. He emitted a whistling moan that resembled a death rattle.

The dogs that chased her earlier in the day crept from the shadows. They sat at their master's side, watching her. Blood-tinged saliva dripped from their jowls.

Martha sobbed and mumbled incoherently. The Ice Man drew a short-handled sickle from within his coat and flicked his wrist. The blade sliced through her neck, and Martha slumped to the floor. He released his dogs, and they eagerly lapped up the warm crimson puddle forming on the floor.

When they had drunk their fill, he bagged Martha's corpse and dragged it to a black sleigh hidden behind the house. After harnessing the thick, muscular dogs, he cracked his whip. Wild howls carried in the wind while the dogs took to the sky on another paralyzing and frigid tempest.

The Ice Man drove his dogs toward the next town to collect more souls as Earth's penance to Mother Nature. The humans' time had come to pay for their role in squandering and ravishing her creation, and he had plenty of stops to make.

No Rest for the Weary

Every motel along the winding, coastal highway flashed a "No Vacancy" sign. Merle cursed himself for not making an advance reservation. The nine hour drive exhausted him, and not finding a room had pushed his patience to the limit.

He finally spotted a weathered sign alongside the highway—*Bay View Inn - next turnoff - one mile*. Upon reaching a gravel driveway, he did not hesitate to slow down and turn. He pulled up in front of the office. Small, faded blue bungalows jutted away from it in an L shape.

He stepped into the office. An archway behind the front desk opened up into the manager's living room. A matronly woman watching television from a rocking chair glanced up at him over her glasses.

"You lost, mister?"

"No, but I need a room and thought you might have one available."

She chuckled. "Well, I don't. We're closed for remodeling."

"Look, I drove up from Los Angeles and am exhausted."

She struggled to her feet and hobbled toward him. "Believe me, I would like to rent you a room but most of them are torn up with no carpet or furniture."

Merle pulled a wad of cash from his pocket. He peeled off several twenties and spread them on the counter.

"Look, have you got anything at all I might be able to sleep in for the night? Every motel I tried is booked and it sounds like you could use the money."

She eyed him and then the bills. She scooped them up as though fearing he might change his mind.

"Well, there is a bungalow at the end though it has a broken out window covered over with a sheet of plastic. It will be damp and chilly, and if it rains you'll probably get wet. I won't be responsible should you get hurt or sick."

He grabbed the room key and parked in front of the bungalow. The plastic covering the window was shredded and the strips flapped in the breeze. Merle opened the door and stepped back, gasping.

Three sea birds perched on a tarp covered dresser flapped their wings in a panic. Feathers and droppings scattered in their frenzied escape through the open window.

Tarps covered a faded, cheap quality couch and chair, and a dank, moldy odor rose from the rain-stained carpet. The only bright spot in the room was a large colorful print of an oversized sea bird strutting across a sandy, shell-littered beach. It hung canted on the wall over the dresser.

Merle removed the tarp covering the bed. At least the sheets and bedcovers looked clean and pressed. He plopped onto the mattress and sank into it. After struggling to stand up, he decided to take a shower.

Upon stepping into the bathroom, Merle changed his mind. Rusty water spewed out of the shower spigot, and the dirty tub resembled a wash basin for a mud wrestler. At that moment he wished he wasn't so exhausted; a couple hours in some rest stop parking lot would have been better.

After watching the local news, Merle shut off the TV and crawled into bed. The distant ocean roar and salty breeze wafting through the open window lulled him to sleep. A few hours later a loud crash woke him with an adrenaline rush surging through his body.

"What the hell ...!" Merle hollered, scrambling out of bed.

He flipped on the light and saw that the framed print had fallen to the floor. He leaned it against the couch and returned to bed. A few hours later he was awakened once again by loud scraping in the darkness.

Merle peeked from beneath the covers. A large shadow across the room was approaching him in the darkness.

"Who's there?" he called out.

The darkened blob slammed against his chest as he reached for the nightstand light. Merle fell back onto the bed with the wind knocked out of him. He felt a sudden, stabbing pain and grabbed at his throat.

Warm sticky blood gushing from his neck coated his hands. He gasped for a breath and crawled to his knees though the rapid blood loss weakened him. Merle lay back onto the floor with the coagulating liquid welling up in his throat.

The huge bird hopped onto his chest. It dug into Merle's abdomen with its sharp talons and let out a high-pitched screech. The room filled with seagulls and terns that buffeted each other trying to get through the window.

The odor of damp feathers filled the air while the birds perched on the furniture and crowded onto the bed. They screeched and pecked at each other fighting to climb onto Merle. While they pecked at his torso and extremities, the larger bird stabbed its beak into Merle's eyes.

At dawn the birds flew from the room en masse. Once all the other birds were gone, the larger bird hopped to the floor and strutted across the room. It stepped over the frame and disappeared into the print.

Later that morning, the manager found Merle sprawled across the bed. Feathers littered his disfigured and bloodied corpse. The manager removed what cash and valuables she could find in his clothes and car before calling the police.

While awaiting their arrival, she noticed a trail of crimson splotches that led across the floor and onto the print. They grew smaller until ending where the bird stood pecking at the seashells with its red-tipped beak. Upon closer examination, the bird's beak was splattered in crimson. Her screams dissipated in the salty morning air, heard only by the flock of terns landing in the yard outside the bungalow.

Pest Control

Dante Devereaux gazed out the massive picture window of his suburban New Orleans mansion. The howling winds outside bent a century old magnolia sideways. Any moment, it might snap.

He imagined the sound to be similar to the arm and leg bones of that young prostitute he bedded and hacked to pieces before barbequing earlier in the month. The meat tasted so sweet and tender he'd gnawed into the bone and had to pick the slivers from his palate.

The dinner bell rang, and he retired to the dining room. Ophelia, his maid, had anticipated the coming storm and prepared his favorite meal, French Quarter chili. She used the stew meat he'd cut from the same woman's belly.

Dante learned early on the younger ones' bodies were sweeter and suppler than the older ladies of the night. He discovered the more experienced they were at plying their trade, the more their meat tasted stringy and bland.

He considered himself a cut above the other vampires preying on visitors to New Orleans night clubs and back allies. Most contented themselves with only draining their victims' blood and leaving the corpses to rot. Dante prided himself on minimizing the waste of his victims through cannibalizing, thus leaving little evidence of his handiwork.

As the hall clock tolled nine times, Dante readied himself for another evening of fiendish revelry. His driver dropped him off at a club on Bourbon Street where he met a young woman he'd connected with in an online chat room.

"My dear Angie," he said, handing her a snifter of Anisette. "You are much lovelier than you described yourself."

"Merci Beaucoup, Monsieur Devereaux," she replied. "And may I say you are much more handsome than I imagined."

Her nostrils flared while she sipped her Anisette and savored its tart licorice taste. They talked and laughed into the night, relaxed and enjoying each other's company.

Dante moved closer and nuzzled the nape of her neck. The intoxicating scent of her perfume drove him crazy with desire and he struggled to contain himself from biting her neck right there in the club. Shortly after midnight Dante suggested they return to his mansion.

She smiled wickedly. "Ooh, you are such a naughty boy. I may have to punish you."

"My lovely Angie," Dante replied, "I can't wait. Tell me what you intend to do."

"Let's wait." She cooed and nibbled on his ear. "Let it be a surprise."

Angie slung her embroidered silk purse over her shoulder as they strolled to his car. Dante saw that it appeared heavy and reached to carry it for her.

"Let me take that for you," he said.

Instead, she locked her arm through his and playfully replied, "No, no, no my love. I have toys for us to play with, and I want them to be a surprise."

****

Upon returning to his mansion, Dante led her into the parlor. She excused herself to the bathroom, and returned a few minutes later wearing a black nightgown of criss-crossed leather straps exposing all but the most intimate parts of her body.

"Your beauty defies description," he said, nearly breathless. He pointed to the bar and continued, "Please pour us each a snifter of Cognac while I stoke the fire."

When they sat on the couch, Dante ran his hand along her slender leg, lingering on the softness of her inner thigh.

"My dearest Angie," he said. "Your scent is driving me crazy and I want to fill you with passion you've never known."

"Then, we shall finish our drink," she replied, her voice evocative and breathless. "We shall drive each other insane with passion."

Moments later, Dante's cheeks went numb. His eyes felt gritty and the room spun. His arms and legs jerked involuntarily. Angie said something, but her words sounded choppy and garbled.

She dragged him to the table and laid him on his back. He wanted to pull away and call out, but had lost all feeling in his extremities.

A deep burn settled in Dante's chest. Angie leaned over slightly and gazed into his eyes. Through the drug-induced haze, he could make out her smiling face and the glint of something metallic in her hand.

The room faded into darkness. Dante never felt her remove his heart or saw her eyes roll up into their sockets enraptured as she bit into it.

****

The next morning, Ophelia discovered Dante's remains and called the police. After an extensive investigation, they labeled the case unresolved and closed it. As they had in several other similar homicides of suspected vampires, there were no prints or evidence other than his mutilated body.

All the police knew was that whenever this happened, Crescent City's homicide rate and missing persons' reports temporarily declined.

Reparation

The pot roast aroma wafted up the stairs from the kitchen, reminding Caleb his dinner guest would be arriving soon. He hadn't seen Marguerite in twenty years. They were high school sweethearts and once talked of marrying after graduating from college.

They vowed to see each other during semester breaks and holidays, though their long distance relationship and studies ultimately led to their breaking up. She wanted to change the world and opted for an indigenous people's research program. Upon being awarded a research grant, she traveled to Guatemala, though a year later her team disappeared in the deep jungle.

They weren't found. Caleb got on with his life, but never married. Several years later, a news story reported that an American construction firm deforesting a tract of land in the jungle found Marguerite. The media called it a miracle though she required lengthy hospitalization for malnutrition, exhaustion, and emotional trauma.

When Caleb called her family wanting to see her upon her return home, they said she was having a difficult time readjusting and would call him when she was ready. He could barely contain his excitement when she finally called. They talked for over an hour and he felt on top of the world when she accepted his invitation for dinner.

****

Caleb's hands shook while he uncorked the wine. He wondered how she would look after all this time and whether there still might be a spark between them. When the doorbell rang, he nearly knocked the bottle over hurrying to the door.

Upon opening it, he disguised his shock with a broad smile. Marguerite's thick auburn hair had turned wiry and gray, and her sparkling, hazel eyes now sat dark and muddied in their hollow sockets. She walked with a stilted gait that barely supported her emaciated frame.

He wrapped his arms around her in a gentle hug. "My God, you look great."

"You're too kind," she said, sounding raspy and weak. "I know I look dreadful."

"Not to me," he replied. After leading her into the living room, he continued, "I wish things could have been different."

"Me, too," she replied, "and I'm thrilled you took the time to contact me."

Marguerite wrapped her arms around him and gave him a passionate kiss, catching him off guard. Her tongue darted between his lips and intertwined with his. Caleb nearly gagged from the saliva building up in his mouth.

With they finally broke the kiss; he discreetly swallowed the saliva she'd left in his mouth. Marguerite stared into his eyes and stroked her hand against his cheek. Caleb poured her a glass of wine.

"I'm sorry," she said, her face flushed in a pinkish glow. "I guess I got carried away. I cannot remember how long it's been since I have been with a man."

"That's alright," he said, smiling. "I certainly didn't mind."

During supper, their conversation turned to her travels to Central America. As she described the work she did with the tribes, Marguerite's tone of voice changed.

She began to rant about how the industrial world was destroying the rain forests. Bitterness colored her voice while she lamented how the indigenous tribes' existence was threatened.

"Something needs to be done!" she cried. "Change has to begin on a local level."

Caleb's eyed widened with concern though he nodded politely and refilled her wine glass. Marguerite must have sensed his uneasiness.

"Well, here I am ranting on and on." She softened her tone and raised her glass with a smile. "Here's to coming home."

She emptied her glass and held it out for a refill. All through dinner, she talked nonstop about how she was going to change the world. Caleb just listened and nodded.

Marguerite's voracious appetite surprised him. She gorged herself on the roast and vegetables. Although her pallid and withered appearance did not change, her energy increased.

She curled her lower lip in mock disappointment when he cleared the table. They returned to the living room, and Marguerite slid next to him on the couch.

He nuzzled the soft warmth of her neck and whispered, "This almost feels like when we were in high school."

"Almost," she replied and kissed him.

A sharp pain stabbed at Caleb's belly and he doubled over. She held onto him, rubbing his back.

"Caleb, are you all right?"

"Yeah," he replied, though he had turned pale and his stomach gurgled loudly.

He staggered to his feet and hurried to the bathroom. After bending over the sink for a sip of cold water, he straightened up. Caleb gasped and stepped backward staring into the mirror.

His face now appeared pasty gray and his eyes had sunk seep into their sockets. Droplets of blood trickled down his cheeks like tears. A sharp pain jerked his head back and his eyes rolled up into his skull.

Caleb fell to the floor and began to seize. Bloodied foam gurgled up from his throat while he gnashed his teeth and spit out pieces of his tongue.

Marguerite stepped through the doorway. His limp body lay at her feet, and he was shriveling up as though being consumed from within. She smiled as inch-long, beetle-like insects from the Central American jungle began swarming out of his orifices.

The egg sac she placed into Caleb's mouth with her saliva had hatched. Marguerite's debt was now paid. Her captors' tribal elders spared her when she agreed to use the eggs to help destroy the civilized world for its inhumanity.

This was the tribe's reparation for the devastation of their rain forest. Marguerite had explained to the elders that if they wanted to change the world, it would have to be on a local level.

The creatures skittered out through the door and into the street. They would be ingested by Caleb's neighbors while they slept, and once they hatched, the process would begin again, and again, and again …

Love Letters

Cheryl had been missing three months when Ben decided to stop grieving and travel. Besides, he had grown tired of trying to convince the insurance company he had nothing to do with her disappearance and that his claim was valid.

Even the police, who initially suspected him, removed Ben from their suspect list after grilling him numerous times. Thankfully, friends and neighbors corroborated Ben's statements regarding Carol's unhappiness in the relationship, and the police accepted that she left of her own volition.

However, the insurance company announced they would not settle the $250,000 claim on the policy Ben took out on Cheryl after their wedding until they were convinced she was legally dead.

That was fine with him, as he had enough money socked away, at least for a while. It was just that the policy would make for a tidy little nest egg.

Ben decided to clean the clutter in the house, and then pack. If Cheryl were here now, her barrage of criticism and nagging about picking up dirty underwear, washing the dirty dishes piled up in the kitchen, and leaving the toilet seat up would be unrelenting. However, since she was not there, it didn't matter.

He started in his office, sorting through a 24-inch high stack of papers on his desk. Midway down, Ben found an official looking unopened letter from Cheryl sticking out just enough to be noticed. It was neatly typed and dated a few days before she disappeared.

They had several tumultuous arguments around that time and once or twice Carol had resorted to hurling coffee cups, ashtrays, and books. He still had a small bruise above his ear from *War and Peace*.

Ben removed the letter and read it.

> *"Dearest Ben,*
>
> *After reading this, please enjoy a bottle of homemade wine I hid for you in the kitchen cupboard. I know we've had our differences, so consider this something of an olive leaf.*
>
> *Cheryl."*

Well, at least she left him something to enjoy besides her absence. Ben respected her ability to craft a fine wine; Cheryl's chemistry degree provided her the wherewithal to maximize the flavor and give it a good alcohol kick.

He retrieved the bottle and found another letter attached to it. The faint aroma of her favorite perfume emanated from the faded pink letterhead inside the envelope.

He poured a glass and admired its reddish-plum hue. Its thick, sweet taste reminded him of a fine dessert wine.

"Not bad, Cheryl," he said, "not bad."

Then, he read her letter.

Ben,

By the time you read this, you will have already killed me. I suppose I should be angry with you, but I'm not.

I had not told you, but during my visit to Dr. Olds a month ago, I was diagnosed with terminal pancreatic cancer. I would have died a painful death anyway, so for that, I thank you.

But, you scheming, no-good bastard, I knew you would kill me if you got the chance and make a joke of what I'd once considered a sacred marriage.

Well, two can play that game, buddy. Instead of divorcing, I wanted to ensure you never forgot me as long as you lived. I think I have done that, so at least enjoy the wine I originally made for our anniversary.

By the way, in the far corner of the basement by the hole you were digging for my wine cellar, I hid another bottle for you to share with whoever your new flavor of the week bitch might be.

Cheryl

Ben shook his head and smiled. Had she really been that stupid to think he dug the hole for a wine cellar?

His stomach gurgled and roiled as he cantered down the stairs. He remembered he had not eaten all day, and decided to go back upstairs and grab a bite after retrieving the next bottle. His nostrils flared from the cellar's dank, musty odor.

He smirked at the framed photo of Cheryl that sat on the end table and dropped to his knees. After rolling back the carpeting in front of the couch and end table, he rapped on the concrete with his knuckles.

"Hello, anyone there?" he asked. "Hmm, I guess not. You know Cheryl, I didn't realize it before but the color of the concrete covering the hole and your body almost matches the rest of the floor. You would be pleased."

He felt slightly flush and his skin clammy as he kicked the carpet back in place. After retrieving the third bottle and letter, he sat on the couch and read it.

Dear Ben,

You didn't really think I would let you get away with murder, did you? I was not the bimbo you made me out to be. As you read this you probably are feeling a bit queasy, which is normal.

There is no easy way to put this, so I will give it to you straight. I laced all three bottles of wine with a heavy dose of strychnine. Therefore, if you haven't already, you will soon convulse and lapse into a coma.

I know that you are most likely reading this in the basement alone. You always were a dumb ass, though not dumb enough to tell anyone you killed me.

However, you will not make it out of the cellar alive and perhaps even rot before anyone finds you. Therefore, my dear Benjamin, enjoy.

See you in Hell,

Cheryl

"You bitch!"

Ben cast a hateful stare at the floor and crumpled the letter. He jumped from the couch and started for the stairs, but doubled over in pain. His insides felt as though they were twisting into a knot, and the acidic taste of bile rose in his throat. He projectile-vomited across the room and collapsed onto the end table. The table broke into pieces, and he landed face first on the shattered glass and frame that held Cheryl's smiling photo.

Glass shards sliced into his paling face, and blood pooled beneath him. Ben's eyes cast a lifeless gaze into the photo and the room dissipated into darkness. As Ben's fixed gaze turned lifeless and dark, a faint sound that resembled muffled laughter echoed from beneath the floor.

One Way or Another

Dorothy had the cab driver pull into the driveway. After a voluntary commitment to the state hospital, she was returning home. When her childhood fear of the dark and the boogieman continued into college, she knew she needed either deep therapy or in-patient treatment. She opted for the latter.

She shivered in the chilly fall wind as she stepped from the cab feeling triumphant. While she hadn't been cured, at least the staff provided her with the mental tools to cope with her mind monsters. She had no idea how long outpatient therapy would last, but felt optimistic about its outcome.

As Dorothy carried her suitcase toward the house, she caught a glimpse of movement in the late afternoon shadows near a thick bush. She quelled her apprehension using a fear suppression method learned during treatment. Once relaxed, she crossed the lawn to the side of the house.

"Hello, can I help you?" she called out, stepping around the corner.

She saw nothing but gloomy afternoon shadows. She returned to the front door and wriggled her key into the lock. *How silly it all seems now,* she thought, *that I had allowed a shadowy, nonexistent creature to control me.*

Upon stepping inside, she hollered, "Hey, you guys, I'm home!"

Seconds later her mother's voice echoed down from upstairs, "Dorothy!"

Her footsteps thumped on the stairs as she hurried down to hug her daughter. "We weren't expecting you for at least another week. I've been using your room for sewing and storage, and haven't even cleaned it out yet."

Her mother's averted gaze seemed to signal apprehension about broaching the subject of Dorothy's hospital stay.

"That's all right, Mom, I'll sleep on the couch for a day or two. It's super comfortable anyway."

"I wish we would have known you were coming so soon. We already made plans to have dinner with the Hendersons across town, and won't be home until late. I'm sure they would love to see you though; why don't you join us?"

"No, go have fun. It'll give me a chance to unwind and enjoy the quiet," Dorothy said.

After her parents left, Dorothy lit the gas fireplace and grabbed an afghan from a wicker basket by the hearth. A pumpkin spice candle flickered on the end table. Its relaxing aroma conjured the false, yet romantic textbook images of Pilgrims and their arrival in the new world, something her freshman college professor promptly debunked. Dorothy chuckled to herself that Halloween was barely over and her mom had wasted no time setting out the Thanksgiving decorations.

As she immersed herself into her book, a draft of chilly air flooded her arms with goose bumps. Dorothy snuggled beneath the blanket, comforted by the familiar surroundings of home. Outside, the whistle and moan of a chilly north wind rattled the windows.

Several minutes later, she sat up as something scratched at the windows. *Branches in the wind,* she thought, though the downy hairs on her neck bristled. The unsettling feelings prompted her to do as she'd learned, be proactive and diffuse the fear. Dorothy grabbed a carving knife from its butcher block holder on the kitchen counter, then hurried back to the couch.

She frowned at her childish behavior and chided herself, "Oh, good God, Dorothy, quit acting like a damn child! You're home safe."

After sliding the knife between the cushion and arm rest, she changed the channel to a classical music station and delved into her novel.

An hour later, she twitched with the uneasy feeling someone was watching her. She went to the window, but saw only the chilly night. At that moment, Dorothy forgot all she learned and began to panic.

After running from room to room locking windows and shutting blinds, she grabbed the phone to call the police. She hung up though; if they responded and learned she had just been released from the state hospital, they would think she was nuts for calling them to come investigate.

A little later, Dorothy heard a thud upstairs as though something bumped the wall. She wrapped her fingers around the knife handle and tiptoed to the stairs. She flipped the light switch and raised the knife.

"Damn it, Mom!" she hollered, dropping her arm and staring up the stairs. "Did you have to put a frigging coat and hat tree at the top of the stairs?"

Dorothy returned to the couch, her heart pounding and hands shaking. After a series of deep breathing exercises, she settled down enough to read.

She drifted off to sleep and awakened two hours later by tickling on her neck. *An unruly strand of hair,* she thought, and brushed at her neck. The tickle remained and Dorothy jumped to her feet.

Dorothy turned her attention to the feeling that something was now crawling on her leg. After she kicked off her blue jeans, it appeared there were things crawling beneath the skin on her legs. As she raked her fingernails across her legs, she felt movement in her belly.

Whatever it was seemed to be eating its way through her belly. Bile rose in her throat and Dorothy vomited a handful of thick slugs. She grabbed the knife from its slot in the couch and stabbed at her rippling belly repeatedly.

Her hysterical screams filled the room as blood splattered the walls and furniture. Dorothy finally collapsed into a dark crimson pool. Her legs twitched for several seconds, then stopped.

A soft, sinister laugh broke the silence. An opaque, featureless creature inside a shifting cloak-like shadow took shape. The Boogie Man appeared and leaned toward Dorothy. He placed his lips on hers and sucked out her soul.

****

When she was a child, he crept up to her bed one night and whispered in her ear that one way or another he would someday collect her soul. Upon her return home, he saw that she was still vulnerable in spite of her so-called treatment. There had been no better time to act.

"Come children, we are needed elsewhere," he said, drawing the slugs into the darkness swirling around him.

Shortly afterward, headlights swept past the windows and a car pulled into the driveway. The Boogie Man retreated into the swirling, diaphanous darkness with Dorothy's soul.

Her twisted and bloodied corpse lay in the dark as another victim of suicide or murder, never to hear the horrific screams that would soon break the silence.

Redemption

Cow pastures, wheat fields, and sheep grazing on sun-dried patches of wild grass decorated the desolate roads between towns. The drive through Iowa and into Nebraska had been long and tedious. Arnie's fatigued eyes drooped and he cursed himself for not arranging for a motel room in advance.

He passed a weathered road sign that read, "To him resign your fate; tomorrow will be too late. Why not rest in Redemption?"

Several miles down the road, he entered the town limits of Redemption. Arnie breathed a sigh of relief that the sign referred to a real town and not a metaphor.

As he followed the main street into town, he could not help but notice how the picture book town instilled a feeling of tranquility. Well-kept, clapboard houses surrounded by lilac bushes and white fences lined Main Street, as did aging elm trees with wide trunks and canopies that shaded the entire neighborhood.

He drove past a blue and white building with a neon sign that said, "The Moonlight Café: Home Cooking at its Best," His stomach gurgled with hunger, though he drove on looking for a motel. A block away, he spotted a blinking motel sign with its "vacancy" sign lit.

His chest heaved with a sigh of relief as he pulled in and trudged into the office.

After checking in, he walked several blocks back to the café. Every store he passed was closed for the day, though a crowd of people had converged on the city park a block over. *Most of the town must be there,* he thought.

Arnie quickened his pace, fearing that the restaurant would be closed. A sign in the window allayed his fears when he read, *Help us celebrate Redemption Days! 6PM at the city park bandstand; the barbeque is on us.*

As he stepped through the door, his mouth watered from the warm aroma of fresh coffee and pie. Several customers sitting at the counter turned toward the door when its overhead bell tinkled. They stared for a moment before resuming their quiet conversations.

"Hi there," the waitress said, stepping up to the table. "You in town for the celebration?"

"No, I'm just passing through and stopped for the night."

He glanced up at her as she set a menu on the table. The nametag on her starched white blouse read "Martha."

"Well then, you don't want to miss the festivities. We don't do this barbeque very often, but when we do, it's a real biggie. The city park bandstand sits across the street from the back door. By the way, what's your name?"

"Arnie."

"Well, Arnie, why don't you be my guest?"

Although she had him in age by several years, he figured why not. A free meal and a woman's companionship for a couple hours of time was a fair trade.

"Sounds too good to pass up," he said, smiling up at her. "What time should I come back?"

Martha patted his arm, and giving it a squeeze replied, "You don't even need to leave. I'll fix you a little something to tide you over. You can sit here and sip on your coffee while I drag the salads and beans out of the fridge."

"Sounds good to me."

She started to walk away, and turned back to him. "I hope you don't mind, Arnie, but there is always a little religion thrown in at these events. You know how small towns are."

"I don't mind," he said, "as long as it doesn't go on all night."

"Believe me it won't," she replied. "Listen, after I get the coals going for the barbeque, I could use a little help."

"I'm yours," he said.

She gave him a wink and disappeared into the kitchen. Upon returning with his coffee, she set it in front of him.

"The nights cool off pretty quick so I put a little something in there to ward off the chill."

Arnie took a sip and the warm burn of bourbon slid down his throat. Martha left as her counter customers awaited her at the cash register. She kept his cup filled between jaunts in and out of the kitchen.

The tantalizing aroma of the oak briquettes burning behind the restaurant wafted through the door and tickled his taste buds. After a few minutes his tired eyes once more sagged over his pupils. He spotted Martha and called to her, slurring his words.

"Oh boy," she said, and started toward him. "I guess you can't hold your liquor too well."

"Nah, it's not that," he said, flashing a dumb smile. "It was a long drive. I guess I'm more tired than I thought."

"Well, sweety, I've got just the remedy for you," she said, and helped him to his feet.

She led him into the kitchen. Arnie's chin bobbed off his chest and when he lifted it to see where she was, the room went black.

****

Arnie awakened in a deep fog with no idea how long he'd been unconscious. He lay on a table outside the café back door and heard a crowd hollering, "Save us from sin, Reverend! We are all sinners and need redemption. "

The Reverend wore a black smock and his deep-set eyes stared toward Arnie like two smoldering cinders. Arnie tried to stand but discovered he was paralyzed and had only the ability to look sideways and up at the sky.

"The world-uh is the Devil's workshop and-uh idle hands do his bidding!" the Reverend replied in a booming voice.

"AMEN!"

The crowd appeared to be in some kind of trance. Some glanced skyward, their faces contorted and their eyes upturned into their lids with an otherworldly stare. Several stood board-rigid with their arms held out in the sign of a crucifix. Others shuddered and gyrated in their rapture.

Outstretched hands raised him into the air horizontally. Arnie recognized the faces of the farmers he saw in the café, and they were carrying him toward the park with his wrists, belly, and legs tied to some kind of pole. He writhed about in a panic trying to free his wrists as the men set the pole on a rack. He turned his head enough to see the townspeople moving toward him, some appearing normal and others still entranced.

"Arnie, we praise you for your sacrifice," the booming voice hollered. "Through you, another year of Redemption is assured for all who reside here."

Arnie screamed in excruciating pain as the flames licked against him from below and engulfed his clothes. The odor of burning flesh and hair stung his nostrils, and in his peripheral vision, he caught a glimpse of Martha standing at the carving table still wearing her apron. A smile crossed her thin lips as she slapped a carving knife blade across a sharpener, and motioned for the residents of Redemption to line up for dinner.

The Winner

Henry sat in the lobby awaiting his appointment with Bell, Booker, and Kandel. The sofa's supple, cream-colored leather enveloped him as though wrapping him in an embrace. The inner office door flew open and a young-looking attorney scurried out of the office, his pale face twisted in fright and confusion.

The secretary glanced up from her monitor long enough to watch his hasty exit.

"What happened to him?" Henry asked the receptionist as she disappeared behind her computer.

"They fired him."

"Why?"

"Because we, I mean the firm ALWAYS win, in court as well as every other facet of the profession. They won't tolerate anyone losing a case."

The prestigious criminal law firm had a reputation for seldom losing in court. Henry ignored the admonitions of other firms that Bell, Booker, and Kandel had done so only because they'd made a pact with the devil. But Henry was determined to work for winners, and BBK were winners.

She led Henry into an ornate conference room. Several partners sat around a massive conference table, each perusing a manila file he concluded was his application. They grilled him for hours, covering subjects from his childhood fears to his sex life. No need to discuss his legal expertise, they said. They knew all about him.

****

Three days later, Henry was hired and a welcoming reception was held in his honor. That evening as he headed toward the bar, Henry felt a slap on the shoulder.

"You must be Henry."

"Yes, sir," Henry replied. He turned toward the voice and extended his hand. "And, you are?"

The man ignored his hand. "Gordon Alchemy, senior partner. Welcome aboard."

"Thank you, sir."

"I wasn't at your interview, though I know all about you. Listen, I'd like a word with you in private."

"Absolutely, sir."

Henry followed Gordon to the firm's legal library.

"Do I frighten you?" he asked, curling his lips in a sinister smile. "I've found that most new hires are terrified of me."

"Should I be?" Henry said, not wanting to sound as intimidated as he felt.

"It depends on how committed you are to winning."

Henry's intestines twisted tightly, and his smile disappeared.

"I'm very committed, sir."

The library floor began to descend and Henry trembled inside, unsure what was happening. Gordon however ignored it and eyed Henry with an astute stare, as though sizing him up. "That's an Interview 101 answer. Let me ask again, how committed are you to winning?"

"I'm prepared to do whatever it takes to win, sir."

"Yes, whatever it takes. I trust you did your homework about the firm?"

"Most certainly; the firm's success rate is nearly flawless."

"Correct. We almost always win! Like a good shepherd, we keep a close eye on our flock. If an attorney loses his edge, we take immediate steps to rectify the situation."

"I understand that, sir."

"Don't interrupt me." Henry squirmed as Gordon's jaw tightened. "We're highly specialized, and judges like us for our expediency in helping rid the city of crime."

"B-but, how is consistently getting accused criminals off the hook stopping crime?"

"Because we ensure they never commit another one."

The library floor jerked to a stop. They stepped out the door and into a dark, icy room that smelled of decay. Meat hooks wound their way along the ceiling on a conveyer chain leading to a steel freezer against the wall.

"What's all this?" Henry asked.

Gordon slid open the freezer door. Frozen, gutted corpses hung on hooks. Henry fought the urge to vomit and wondered what the hell he'd gotten himself into.

"This is where we put the scum of the city on ice until they can be disposed of properly."

After returning to the library, Gordon put his hand on Henry's shoulder, and looked him in the eye. Henry winced as his fingernails dug through his suit coat into the skin.

"Should you ever betray the firm or lose a case, let's just say you'll be put on ice as well."

"I'll do my best, sir," he said, fighting back the urge to vomit.

****

In the following months however, Henry developed a reputation as a hardnosed defender. A year later though, a client accused of several grisly murders was found guilty of lesser charges, and sentenced to three years. With good behavior, the scum would be out on the streets within eighteen months.

Gordon sat in the rear of the courtroom, glaring at Henry contemptuously. As soon as court adjourned, the young jurist ran like hell to his car and sped home. During the drive, however, Henry heard the constant shriek of a banshee and scratching on the car's roof.

Once home, he locked the doors and windows, and crouched in a darkened corner with a loaded shotgun. The banshee circled the house looking for an entrance. Then, Henry inhaled the stench of death.

He turned as the firm's receptionist, transformed into a banshee wafted into the room through the fireplace. Her diaphanous, silk gown flowed behind her while she hovered overhead and pressed her rotting, snarling face up close to Henry's.

His heart sank with the realization he'd left the flue open. Before he could react, her razor honed fingernails ripped into his flesh as if it was tissue paper. Henry's final thought was of her statement the day he interviewed for the job: the firm always won.

The Orchard

"Do you really believe that crap?" Max asked the realtor when he divulged a local legend regarding the farm he wanted to buy.

The realtor just chuckled and replied, "As surreal as it sounds, I'm required to provide full disclosure on any adverse history, real or not."

The story passed from generation to generation told of a Hessian soldier homesteading the farm at the end of the revolutionary war. He planted an apple orchard between his fields and a stand of oak trees, and was said to have put a curse on the woods to punish anyone trying to sneak through the trees to steal his apples. One day the Hessian entered the woods and disappeared.

During the Great Depression, rumors spread about hobos disappearing from an encampment built in the woods near a now defunct rail line. In the fifties, local teens intrigued by the stories flocked to the woods hunting bogeymen, ghosts, and monstrous eyes glowing in the dark, and drinking beer as a rite of passage.

When a few kids went missing, searches came up empty, though no evidence of foul play was found. The sheriff concluded the woods' close proximity to the tracks provided ample opportunity to hop a freight train and run away on an adventure. He said they would probably return soon, though none did.

Max figured the hobos generated the rumors as a hoax to scare people and keep them away from the encampment. In spite of the stories, he bought the farm and all its acreage. An agricultural cooperative leased most of the acreage. He retained the woods, orchard, and several acres for a hobby farm.

The lease income from the cooperative would pay his bills, the lumber from the oak trees would generate a nice profit, and apples from trees in the fall reeked of Americana; they couldn't help but make money.

****

After settling in, Max drove to the rear of the property to find the old hobo camp. Once he cleared the woods and whatever was left of the camp, he would dispel the rumors once and for all.

He followed an access road running alongside the tracks. After parking, Max walked the tree line. Next to the remnants of a weed-covered path he found a tree with three weathered, diagonal lines carved into the trunk; it was a hobo sign signaling others passing through that the site was unsafe.

He followed the path into the woods and found remnants of the old encampment tucked under the trees' thick canopy. The eerie quiet was broken only by a lone hoot owl's call and a breeze rustling through the trees. He found only a few wood scraps scattered among the overgrown weeds, some rusted cans and a rusty, dented caldron.

He discovered several trees with patches of bark stripped away. They revealed huge, twisted knots artfully carved with human cameos. Max figured they were vagabonds immortalized by a fellow hobo artist.

Max set out for the orchard and nearly tripped over the exposed and twisted roots from the oak trees. Upon reaching the clearing, his heart sank. The orchard had not been tended to in some time and needed a lot of work. Still, when he grabbed an apple off the branch and bit into it, its tart sweetness pleased and surprised him.

Twilight set in and Max retraced his steps toward the car. All around him leaves rustled and the oak limbs creaked in a breeze that began to blow. Twigs snapped behind him and he turned quickly, thinking someone might be following him.

"Who's out there?" he called, but received no reply.

Max broke into a jog. By the time he reached the hobo encampment, he was chastising himself for letting the forest sounds instill a twinge of childish fear into his psyche.

He slowed down and pushed a low-hanging branch out of his way. Another branch hooked to it dislodged and snapped forward, smacking Max in the forehead like a whip.

He stepped back, stunned, and tripped over an exposed tree root. He staggered to his feet and rubbed at the welt streaking across his forehead.

The roots rose from the ground and sprouted narrow, centipede-like tentacles that stretched out and whipped around his legs. Max kicked with a fury and broke free. He started to run but stopped, stunned by the trees with the etched images surrounding him.

Their branches spread low and transformed into skeletal, bark-covered arms. The carved images transformed into the faces of rotted corpses and the air hung heavy with the sickly stench of decay. Max screamed for help as their outstretched arms pulled him against an adjacent oak's barren strip of trunk.

Sap oozing out of the wood enveloped him and drew him into the thick syrupy pulp. While the tree dissolved and absorbed him, Max's bones crunched and joints popped from their sockets. His bloodcurdling screams ceased as he disappeared into the tree, leaving only his image etched into the trunk.

****

A year later, a couple of high school kids entered the woods. The boy spotted an old shoe hanging on a stubby branch that resembled part of a skeletal foot sticking out of an etched strip of trunk.

"Cool!" he said, "Somebody carved some really neat images in these trees."

The girl shivered and tugged his arm. "C'mon, let's go to the orchard. This place gives me the creeps and I feel like someone's watching us."

They continued toward the orchard, and the two young trees flanking Max's reached down and stripped the bark away from a section of their trunks. The unbleached patches glistened with a light haze of ooze. Their branches swayed in the breeze, awaiting the teens' return with the impatience of children anticipating Christmas.

Trick or Treat

Jennifer stood at the front door watching the last of the trick or treat super heroes and goblins disappear into the night. Shadows danced off the streetlights in an eerie undulating dance across the sidewalks and yards. After extinguishing the jack o' lantern candles on the porch, she retired for the night.

Marco, her husband, had gone to bed an hour earlier after polishing off the last of his twelve-pack of Rolling Rock. She slid under the covers next to him and reached for him.

He yanked his shoulder away and grumbled, "Don't bother me, bitch. I'm trying to sleep."

"Well, screw you," she replied, and rolled over.

She curled up in a fetal position facing away from him. An hour later, she rolled over and nudged his shoulder.

"What?" he mumbled, burying his head beneath the covers.

"I hear a scraping noise downstairs and think maybe someone's trying to break in."

Marco sat up and cocked his head. "I don't hear anything. Go back to sleep."

Her hand trembled as she grabbed his arm. "No, listen! There's someone at the door!"

Marco pulled the covers over his head. "So, go down and see who the hell it is. I'm tired."

"Me? You're going to make me go down there!" Jennifer fired back. "Oh, what a big man! You won't even protect your wife, and want her to take care of it if someone's breaking in."

"You are such an ass," Jennifer growled.

She swung her legs over the edge of the bed and donned her slippers before tiptoeing down the stairs. After seeing no one there when she peeked through the windows and the front door peephole, Jennifer put her ear to the door and listened. Hearing only silence, she shrugged and returned to bed.

"There was nothing there," Jennifer said, and pulled the covers over her head. "It must have been the wind. But what a sorry excuse for a husband you are."

A little while later, she sat up once again. This time, she heard loud scratching, along with shaking of the door handle.

Jennifer shook his shoulder and said, "All right you jerk, someone's at the door! It's your turn to go down and check it out."

"Damn it!" Marco climbed out of bed. "Who the hell's rude enough to bother someone in the middle of the night?"

"It'll probably be no one, just like when I went down, brave guy."

Marco trudged down the stairs to the front door. He stepped onto the porch and searched the yard. After peering up and down the street and seeing no one, Marco turned to go back inside. A strange putrid odor wafted from behind him down his back.

He spun around and muttered, "Oh, it's you; why the hell haven't you ...?"

A hulking man with a disfigured face stepped from the shadows and a loud "thwack" echoed across the yard. The axe blade hit Marco between the eyes, splitting his head down the middle like firewood.

Jennifer heard the commotion and crept to the top of the stairs. "Honey, is everything okay?"

The man stood out of her line of sight, but waved a hand in the doorway where she could see it.

"Yes, it's done," he said. "You can come down now."

"Oh, okay," she said, sounding relieved. "Thank God it's over. I'm finally free of that no good lout."

Jennifer closed her robe around her and descended the stairs. When she walked through the door, the man stepped from the shadows, startling her. She jumped back, with a hand to her throat.

"Oh, my God!" she cried. "Where did you dig up that godawful mask? I'm surprised you could see well enough to pull this off."

He stepped aside, giving her a clear view of Marco lying on the porch. Jennifer's stood stunned as blood spurted from his head and formed a crimson pool.

"Wow, you sure did a number on him," she said. "That insurance money is going to come in real handy."

"By the way, what's your name again?" Jennifer asked.

"Jason," he replied and removed his mask

She shifted her gaze from Marco to Jason's. Her jaw dropped and her eyes bulged in terror as his axe swung toward her like a baseball bat. Jennifer's head hit the ground spinning like a roulette wheel.

Although the down-payment checks they each sent to his online Craigslist P.O. Box had cleared, Jason had insisted on collecting the balance in person. He removed the cashiers' checks from their individual pajama pockets. After examining them he slid them into his pocket, chuckling at how each paid him to kill the other. He strolled down the steps and into the night resting his axe on his shoulder.

Revenge

An hour after the last Halloween goblin hollered, "Trick or treat," Steve heard something scrape against the outside of the house. He listened a moment and dismissed it as the side yard oak tree's branches scraping against the siding. A Harvest moon flickered as it shone through the window from behind the tree's swaying, skeletal branches.

The thought also crossed his mind that the sound could have come from the older teens that knocked on his door earlier that evening, asking for candy. When he refused, they walked away grumbling about what an asshole he was.

That did not bother him so much; hell, he'd done the same thing when he was their age. The difference between then and now though, was that his Halloween shenanigans consisted of egging cars, soaping windows, or smashing the jack-o'-lanterns. Now, creepy people handed out candy tainted with poisons and razor blades in order to inflict pain on young revelers, and young hoodlums like those teenagers beat up younger kids for their candy and maliciously damaged property. Halloween had become a time of trepidation rather than enjoyment.

The high-pitched screech of a cat followed a heavy thud that reverberated off the side of the house. It sounded like his cat Bingo and Steve jumped from his chair. He bolted toward the window as a dark, opaque shadow flashed past the pane.

After grabbing his pellet gun from the desk drawer, Steve ran outside holding the gun along his thigh, ready to pepper whoever was messing with his cat. Although he found the side yard empty, and heard only the breeze through the trees, a putrid odor wafted his way.

He shone the flashlight beam around the tree, but saw no sign that anyone had been there. When he swept the beam along the side of the house, he saw Bingo lying crouched on the carpet of leaves as though stalking something.

The old tom loved to roam the neighbors' yards and gardens at night stalking birds, rodents, or anything else it could call prey. Steve never minded his nighttime absence, though the bird and critter carcasses scattered about the yard each morning were becoming a problem.

"Come on, Bingo," he said. "Here kitty, it's time to go inside!"

The cat didn't move and Steve walked over to pick him up. He slid one hand beneath the head and the other beneath the hindquarters. The cat lay limp and a warm and sticky liquid oozed between his fingers from a gaping wound in Bingo's side.

"Where are you, you son of a bitch?" He screamed and stood glaring into the shadows. Once again, he saw no one.

Steve bagged Bingo's corpse with a trashcan liner retrieved from the kitchen. He carried it across the yard and into the alley. Beady, reddish eyes along the edge of a dumpster scattered into the darkness the moment the light reflected in their eyes.

After setting the trash bag into the bin, he crossed the alley and stepped back into his yard. He had not yet reached mid-yard when something moving–across the garage roof startled him. Steve swept the flashlight along the roofline but saw nothing. The bushes beside the garage rustled, and he spun toward them in time to catch a brief glimpse of movement in the deep shadows.

He pointed the pellet gun into the darkness and fired several times. "Who's there? Show yourself!"

A search of the yard came up empty. As Steve started toward the house, a tree branch behind him snapped. The same smell he found at the side of the house once again stung his nostrils. Before he could turn, something slammed against his back and his lungs deflated with a loud "Hunnh!"

The pellet gun flew from his hand and he fell face first to the ground. While he lay dazed and gasping for breath, a large black, hazy figure hovered over him. Steve glanced up trying to clear the cloudiness from his brain.

As his vision cleared, his eyes bulged and he gasped in horror. A creature resembling a giant crow stood over him, and peered down at him through huge eyes as colorless as glazed chalk. Numerous gouges where feathers and skin once grew marred the quivering black wings folded against his back.

"Get off me, jerk!" he yelled, thinking it might be one of the teenagers trying to scare him. Within seconds, Steve realized the creature though was anything but human. His insides roiled and nausea rose in his throat when he spotted a clump of Bingo's flesh and tawny fur dangling from one corner of its scarred beak.

Steve scrambled to his feet and found himself surrounded by human sized rodents and birds that had emerged from the shadows. They cut off all avenues of escape.

The crow's tongue clicked with an angry hiss and it raked a clawed foot across Steve's belly. He fell back onto the ground with his steaming entrails sliding out of his abdominal cavity. The creatures' gratified caws and screeches drowned out his horrific screams as the crow's skeletal beak impaled his forehead.

The crow pecked at him several times before unleashing a wraithlike shriek. It flapped its wings and disappeared into the night sky. Bingo's former prey swarmed Steve's corpse, eager to enjoy the feast provided by their feathered avenger.

The Companion

The postal worker thought it odd when he found two weeks of letters and junk mail still stuffed into Mr. Arnold's mailbox. The old man had never let mail pile up like that before. He figured something was wrong and crossed the porch to the front door.

The old man's cat Tabitha lay sphinx-like on the sun-warmed porch watching him through half-closed eyes. The postman stopped to pet her, but thought better of it when a fetid stench emanated from her matted, dirty coat. After several knocks on the door went unanswered, he peeked through the lace-curtained window. The same stench emanated through the windowsill.

He spotted the old man's contorted and decomposing corpse lying at the bottom of the stairs and notified authorities. Police investigators subsequently ruled out foul play, though the corpse had been partially eaten. Smudged, unidentifiable prints led to the pet door in the kitchen.

The coroner's report indicated that the putrefaction probably lured a wild animal, most likely a coyote down from the hills behind the house. Tabitha apparently acquired the odor after lying next to her owner while he lay on the floor decomposing.

****

Several months passed before cleaning and fumigation was completed. The realtor stuck a *For Sale* sign in the yard, though nearly all prospective buyers ended up being nothing more than looky-loos.

After Richard's nasty divorce finally concluded, he had escaped with barely enough money to fund a cheap house. He noticed the listing for the Arnold place was still advertised and that the asking price also included the furniture. Apparently the old man had no heirs and owed no one.

He decided it might be a perfect opportunity to grab a bargain and arranged an appointment to meet the realtor at the house.

As they stood at the base of the stairs, the realtor said, "You know, I'm required by law to provide full disclosure. Mr. Arnold lived alone, except for his cat. He died right here after apparently after a nasty fall down the stairs."

"I know," Richard said. "I read about it in the papers."

"You should also know," she said, "coyotes sometimes sneak down from the foothills and scrounge through the neighborhood. After the old man died, one apparently got into the house and fed on him. If you decide you like the house, you might want to seal off the pet door once you move in."

After inspecting the house, Richard made a ridiculously low offer. The realtor surprised him and accepted, also informing him he could keep whatever furniture he could use. She suggested they complete the paperwork at her office. When they stepped onto the porch, Mr. Arnold's cat Tabitha was laying in her usual place soaking up the afternoon sun. Richard knelt to pet her, but the realtor grabbed his arm.

"I wouldn't do that if I were you. After the old man died, she refused to leave the premises. Every time the animal control officer tried to remove her, she eluded him with a nasty spit and hiss. He even tried tranquilizer darts and pills in her food, but she sensed the danger."

"That's okay," Richard replied. "I'm sure she'll leave when she's ready."

On move-in day, Tabitha lay on the porch. She watched Richard through half-closed eyes while he ferried boxes from the truck into the house. On his final trip the plump, gray cat arched her back in a stretch and waddled toward him.

As she rubbed against his legs and purred, Richard knelt and stroked her thick coat. Within a week, she'd won Richard over and reclaimed her presence in the house. Not long after, she worked her way into sleeping at the foot of Richard's bed.

A few days later, his neighbor knocked on the door.

"I came by to warn you," he said. "Coyotes are coming down from the foothills again. They killed my dog Skippy a couple days ago; I found him partially eaten behind the garage."

"Sorry to hear that," Richard replied. "You think they might be the same ones that fed on old Mr. Arnold?"

His neighbor nodded. "Could be; when they get hungry, they get bold."

That night, Tabitha curled up at the foot of the bed. When Richard awakened the following morning, she had burrowed under his arm and lay sleeping contentedly.

Several nights later, however, he awakened gasping for breath. Tabitha lay stretched across his face. When he pushed her off, she hissed and swiped her claws across his hand.

"Ouch! You little bitch!"

The cat's eyes glowing ember eyes burned into Richard as he grabbed her by the neck. He flung her across the room, and she ricocheted off the wall. As soon as she fled out the door, he hurried into the bathroom, muttering about getting rid of her.

After rinsing off his gouged hand, he started down the darkened stairs to retrieve the first aid kit from the kitchen cabinet. His ankle turned with a loud "pop" and his feet slid out from under him. Richard tumbled down the stairs, taking several cat toys and a hard rubber ball with him.

His head smacked against the banister and steps numerous times, and he came to rest at the base of the stairs unconscious.

He awakened a few hours later to excruciating pain. Jagged fractures protruded though his blood-soaked pajamas, and his broken ribs stabbed at him, making it hard to breathe.

"Someone, help me!" he cried out, only to hear it emerge as a whimper.

Richard remembered his cell phone was lying on top of the buffet. He tried to pull himself across the floor, though the exertion and unbearable pain exhausted him. He laid his head on the floor in submission, thoroughly sapped of his strength.

He caught something moving by the stairs and spotted Tabitha. She sat on the bottom step watching him.

"Please, get out of here," he pleaded in a parched whisper.

The room grew darker and she inched toward him on her belly. Her eyes glowed in angry iridescence. Richard laid his head on the cold tile floor and shut his eyes expecting the worst. Tabitha, however, crawled up to him and licked his face with her rough tongue.

He opened them, and watched in stunned horror as the cat grew larger and larger. Tabitha pinned her ears back and bared her fangs with an evil hiss. Without warning, she lunged.

Richard gurgled and gasped, fighting to take a breath while her claws raked across his throat. His body jerked for several minutes with involuntary spasms while his carotid artery bled out.

Tabitha lapped at the pool of warm blood forming beneath him. Later that evening after clawing open his belly, she fed on his warm, steamy entrails. When she finally waddled up the stairs, her bulging belly scraped across the steps.

Tabitha stretched across Richard's bed and fell asleep. A few days later, Tabitha watched from the top of the stairs while coyotes lured by the stench of decomposition crawled through the pet door.

The Reflection

Sarah followed her fiancé Michael up the aging farmhouse's narrow, attic stairwell. The musty odor of dust and grime rushed out when he opened the door. A single bulb hanging from the ceiling light on a frayed cord provided its dim illumination a few feet past the doorway.

The attic darkness swallowed up the remainder of the room, except for a few dusty shafts of sunlight shining through a transom vent on the far wall. They illuminated a stack of dusty boxes, furniture odds and ends, and a stack of twin bed mattresses and rusty frames crammed together in the middle of the room.

Michael swept his flashlight across the deep shadows framing the room's perimeter. A rat sitting on its hind legs sniffing at the air scrambled out of the light and skittered to safety through a small hole in the wall.

Michael groaned, and batted a cobweb away from his face. "Sarah, this place is a mess; a decaying house with an outdated electrical system and rats. Ka-ching! Ka-ching! No wonder you got it so cheap."

Sarah smiled and shrugged. She had become used to Michael's acidic comments. Besides, she bought the rundown Marsden farmhouse for next to nothing after the realtor explained the farmhouse was abandoned back in the fifties.

The isolated house sat alone for decades, subjected to neglect and deterioration though taxes were kept current by the surrounding, tillable acreage being sublet to a farm co-op. Although the place needed a lot of work, the foundation and frame were sturdy. Sarah had figured that with time and a lot of elbow grease, she and Michael could turn it into their dream home.

The floorboards creaked as she started through the clutter. She gazed around the room. A vanity with matching stool sat where the transom light disappeared into the shadows across the room.

While weaving through the clutter Sarah bumped into a dressmaker's mannequin. The bent frame leaned it toward her, allowing its cold lifeless eyes to stare into hers. She jumped back startled, with a high-pitched gasp.

"Relax, Sarah, it won't bite." Michael said, laughing.

"Damn it, Michael! That's not funny."

Her heart pounded in her chest and she took several slow, deep breaths. Meanwhile Michael turned his attention to a box of knickknacks and an old steamer trunk. He lifted its lid and leaned back, gagging as a dusty, putrid odor escaping the trunk's confines rose toward the ceiling.

"Relax, Michael, it won't bite you!" Sarah called out from across the room.

He rummaged through the trunk and removed a few piles of tattered kids' clothes, a weathered straw farmer's hat, and a pair of coveralls. All were splattered with stiff, brownish stains that looked like paint.

He held the coveralls up, found they looked to be about his size, and on a whim, tried them on. The hat came next. Michael hooked his thumbs through the coverall straps and turned toward Sarah.

"Oh, Sarah," he said, thrusting his hips forward and back suggestively. "Why don't you come here and let your farmer boy plow your field."

Sarah glanced over at him and shuddered at the perverted leer contorting his face.

"Eew! Michael, take those off. You're freaking me out."

She turned her attention back to the dust-caked vanity. The dusty, discolored surface appeared to be slightly warped and distorted her reflection. Sarah leaned toward the surface and ran her fingers across several ripples in the glass.

They seemed to shimmer and the surface warmed to her touch. Sarah felt as though she was being drawn to it. She stood and gazed at Michael in its reflection.

"What do you think, Michael?" she asked, wiggling her ass at him and giggling.

"If I let you plow my field, will you promise to help me turn the attic into a playroom for all our kids?"

Her smile disappeared and she jumped as Michael slammed the trunk lid closed.

"Damn it, Sarah! Are you still hung up on that kid thing?"

"B-but, I thought you wanted a family," she stammered, surprised by his outburst.

"I changed my mind! If you want bratty kids so damn bad, you can stay up here with the little bastards. I sure as hell won't want to deal with them."

In the mirror's reflection she saw Michael crossing the room toward her. His face contorted into an angry unfamiliar glare looking like a man possessed. Sarah held her hand against the mirror and looked back at him over her shoulder.

"Michael, what's gotten into you? Why are you so ...?"

A blinding flash of white light knocked her off balance.

****

Sarah awoke on the floor sprawled across the overturned vanity. A few rays of afternoon sunlight still shone through the transom, though darkness had consumed most of the room. Her head throbbed and she tried to recall what had happened.

The last she remembered was dusting off the vanity. She staggered to her feet, sore and disoriented. Michael didn't answer when she called out to him, and she felt her way through the encroaching shadows toward the door.

Finding the ceiling light off, she pulled the chain. The dim light barely illuminated the dark and cold doorway. Sarah turned the door knob, but discovered it was locked from the outside.

"Damn it, Michael!" she hollered, pounding on it with her fist. "This is not funny. Open up!"

Sarah put her ear to the door. She heard nothing other than silence and her stomach churned with the uneasy feeling something wasn't right. Sudden movement in the shadows caught her eye.

She turned toward it and said, "Michael, quit hiding. I've had enough of your damn games. I want to go home."

"Who are you?" Sarah gasped as instead of Michael, a tall, sullen-faced girl stepped into the dim light.

She continued toward Sarah, walking with a slow, stilted gait. A soiled, shabby frock hung limply on her gaunt frame. The girl remained silent and kept her milky, deep-set eyes fixed on Sarah. In the bulb's dim light patches of decayed skin hung off the girl's pallid face.

"What do you want?" Sarah asked, recoiling.

She spun around, startled by scraping on the floor behind her. Several more emaciated and raggedly dressed children emerged from the shadows. They surrounded her and closed in.

Long, blackened nails tipped their skeletal, pasty fingers while they reached for her.

Sarah screamed and tried to break free when they grabbed her. The more she struggled though, the deeper their brittle fingernails dug into her flesh.

The older girl stepped in and the children stopped. They obediently receded back into the shadows though their eyes remained fixed on Sarah in an iridescent stare.

Sarah flinched when she raised a thin, withered hand toward her face. The girl, however, canted her head and brushed her hand against Sarah's cheek.

Muffled voices in the stairwell broke the silence.

"Michael!" Sarah yelled and started toward the door.

She stopped as several loud whacks splintered the door jamb. It flew open and dusty white light filled the stairwell. A police officer burst through the doorway, sweeping his flashlight and service revolver across the attic.

"Clear!" he hollered.

A pair of detectives entered the room. Michael walked between them, handcuffed. He hesitated at the door and the older detective jerked his arm, pulling him along. The detectives dragged Michael past her without any acknowledgement.

She followed them across the room to the overturned vanity. Sarah felt strangely dispassionate and solemn as she gazed down at the bloated, ashen-faced corpse that had been her. She lay sprawled across the broken vanity, impaled by a large, jagged mirror shard.

"I thought you said on the missing person's report that your fiancé wasn't here when you checked," the detective said.

"I'm telling you she wasn't," Michael replied. "All I remember is we had a spat and I left to cool down. When she didn't come home, I reported her missing."

The younger detective found a pair of bloodstained coveralls lying nearby. He held them up with a latex-gloved hand.

"Hey boss, check this out. Maybe the bloodstains on the bib will match those we found on the shirt at his residence."

"It appears we got us a crime scene here with your name written all over it," the older one said to Michael. He turned toward his partner and continued, "Read him his rights and get him out of here."

The girl stepped from the shadows and gripped Sarah's hand while the uniformed policeman led Michael away. A wispy black shadow in the shape of the hulking, long dead farmer followed them out the door and an aura of serenity and acceptance filled the room.

"So," the younger detective said. "This guy shoved her over the vanity and stabbed her with a mirror shard. That sound about right?"

"Probably," his partner replied. "But I'm not surprised, considering the history of this place. It appears the realtor didn't make a full disclosure."

"What do you mean?"

"Back in '42, a crazed farmer slaughtered his young wife and some runaways and orphans they had taken in. He killed them here in the attic. The papers said the woman threatened to leave him after discovering he was sneaking them into the attic for his own perverted pleasure.

"Reporters called it the crime of the century and rumors abounded of it being haunted. It's been unoccupied ever since, though a couple of vagrants a few years back were found dead downstairs."

****

"We have waited a long time for this," the girl said, speaking for the first time. "Come, everyone; she is going to be our mother now."

The other children stepped from the shadows. They led Sarah across the attic toward a row of assembled twin beds and furniture lining one wall. The detectives shivered in the chilly draft sweeping past in their wake.

The Homecoming

The stranger stood outside the gas station and convenience store door gazing out toward the road. Carl stood at the counter watching the man as he stomped the mud off his boots before stepping through the door. Fog condensation slid off the edge of his wide-brimmed hat and rain slicker, leaving a watery trail from the door to the coffee machine.

"Can I help you?" Carl called out.

"Nope," the stranger replied while he filled a large cup with coffee.

He strode toward the counter and took a long sip of the steaming hot, inky liquid. He gave no indication that it burned his throat when he set it on the counter. Carl's eyes fixed on the wad of mixed denomination bills the man pulled from his pocket.

"Where you headed?" Carl asked as the stranger pulled a couple of dollars from the wad and laid them on the counter.

The stranger said nothing and peered at him through deep set, steely eyes. When he reached inside his rain slicker, Carl shifted his weight uneasily. He relaxed when the man removed a dog-eared map from his raincoat pocket though and spread it across the counter.

"Elm Crest; how much farther is it?"

"You walking or driving?" Carl replied.

The man stepped back and raised his arms, revealing muddy, reddish-brown splatters covering his black knee-length rain slicker.

"Does this answer your question?"

Carl nodded and ran his finger along a narrow blue line.

"Follow this road for about five miles. When you reach a fork in the road, stay to the left and follow it to the interstate. If someone picks you up, Elm Crest will be a forty-five minute ride east."

The man pointed to a squiggly line that made a sharp right at the fork.

"What about this road? It looks a lot shorter."

"It is," Carl replied, "by a good twenty minutes. But most folks around here don't use that road. They call it the highway to hell."

The man stifled a snicker. "Highway to hell, huh? Why is that?"

"A local legend that began thirty or forty years ago said the devil resided on that road because of all the fatalities. There are still crosses where some-occurred."

"So, you believe those deaths were the work of the devil?"'

"Nah," Carl said. "Hell, I live over near Elm Crest and drive that road to work. It's a shortcut, albeit a creepy one. The afternoon shadows falling across the road seem to undulate and distort the turns as though the road is twisting on its own."

"When was the last incident?"

"Maybe ten or fifteen years ago though most folks around here still avoid it."

The stranger chuckled and pulled the brim over his eyes.

"Well, you know what they say; the road to hell is paved with good intentions."

"Ain't it the truth?" Carl replied.

"Nonetheless, I appreciate the information," the man said, walking toward the door.

"Tell you what," Carl said. "If my replacement shows up on time, I'll be heading that way. If you're still on the road, I'll give you a lift."

"I'll probably be long gone by then," the stranger replied.

As soon as he stepped through the door, Carl reached for the .45 caliber pistol he'd placed on the shelf beneath the counter. He pulled back the slide and chambered a round before flipping on the safety.

"I doubt it, buddy," he muttered.

****

Upon reaching the fork in the road, the stranger glanced to the left but headed straight down the two-lane road that ran through the forest. The overcast afternoon sky cast the hillside and landscape in shades of black and gray. The winding road resembled a faded silver ribbon.

"Ooh, the Devil resided here," he smirked, recalling the clerk's warning.

The gravel on the road shoulder crunched beneath his boots while he walked slow and drank in the surrounding land-scape. Upon his reaching the first curve, a chilly damp breeze whistled through the trees. Demonic appearing shadows danced across the pavement.

An hour passed and no traffic approached from either direction. During the last vestiges of twilight, the hum of tires on pavement broke the silence. It grew louder and a dilapidated pickup truck rounded the curve from behind him. As the stranger turned to stick out his thumb, the truck's headlights lit him up.

The driver appeared to head straight for him as if though deliberately wanting to run him over. At the last moment, the truck swerved back into the lane. The truck sped past and then slowed sharply. The driver pulled to a stop along the shoulder, and the growing darkness glowed red from his brake lights.

The driver's side window rolled down and Carl hollered out, "Sorry about that, buddy! The damn truck needs an alignment real bad. My replacement showed up early for once, so hop in."

"Thanks," the stranger said, climbing into the passenger seat.

He stared out the window in silence while Carl pulled back onto the road. Fifteen minutes later, the stranger spoke up.

"How far are we from town?"

Carl nodded toward the road ahead. "Maybe another five miles.

As they approached a sharp curve in the road, Carl slowed the truck. At the same time, he reached for the pistol in his pocket.

"I'll be getting out up here," the stranger said.

"Yeah, I think you're right," Carl replied.

He pulled the gun from his pocket and pointed it toward his passenger. The stranger slammed his boot on Carl's foot. The accelerator hit the floorboard and the truck sped up sharply. At the same time, the stranger grabbed control of the steering wheel.

Carl pulled the trigger and the bullet tore into the rider's face. The wound, however, immediately disappeared and the stranger let out a maniacal laugh. Carl's eyes widened in terror as his passenger's body twisted into a grotesque hulk of muscle and leathery skin.

The stranger's eyes smoldered like blazing cinders and horn-like nubs pushed through the temples of his leathery forehead.

"You should have listened to your own advice and taken the other road," the demon growled. They sped into the curve at seventy miles per hour, and he continued, "I decided to move back home and this is where I will live again."

He yanked the steering wheel hard to the right. The sickening squeal of tires raking across the pavement pierced the air as the pickup skidded sideways off the road. It tumbled end over end into a ravine and burst into flames.

The truck came to rest in an upright inferno. The demon ripped the door off its hinges and stepped out unscathed. He inhaled the thick black smoke filling the air and cast one last look at Carl's charred corpse.

"A-h-h-h! It's good to be home," he bellowed, and disappeared into the murky woods.

About the Contributors

Harold Kempka:

Harold "Hal" Kempka is a former Marine and Vietnam veteran. He resides in the Inland Empire of Southern California with his wife and adopted son. He also has a stepdaughter and two sons from a previous marriage. He's a retired sales representative in the printing paper industry, and covered accounts from Tijuana, Baja California to British Columbia.

Creative writing courses at UC Riverside led him into writing short stories, eventually gravitating toward horror fiction. Hal has had over one hundred and twenty-five flash and short fiction stories published in magazines, e-zines, and anthologies in the US as well as the UK.

Hal is a member of Southern California's Writers Coffeehouse, run by *New York Times* and Multi-Bram Stoker Award winner, Jonathan Maberry.

Teresa Tunaley:

Originating from the UK but residing in the Canary Islands for the last 10 years, freelance artist Teresa Tunaley devotes time to her love of art and painting. For more than 30 years she has been doodling with pencils and dabbling with watercolors. More recently she has been painting traditionally in oil and creating large canvasses full of color and life. Sometimes she uses a more modern technique using software such as Photoshop, Corel Draw and Paint Shop Pro to produce her creations for online publications.

During her art career, she has produced countless illustrations, book covers and paintings. Along with published stories and poetry, she can be credited with award winning cover art and illustrations for author stories. Her work can be seen online and in print across the UK, US, Canada and Europe.

In May 2011, she opened a new Exhibition in Puerto del Santiago (Tenerife, Spain) entitled Tutto per la vita (All for the life). She has over 30 works on show and is hoping to be selected to participate in the Capitals annual Art Festival. Should she win, there will be invitations to exhibit her work in a whirlwind trip across Spain and Italy.

Touching and spectacular "has been the inauguration; Tutto Per la vita" Some thirty of their works appeared, giving you a journey to Spain, Africa, America, Japan and Thailandia. The work was intense with feeling, in full color and textures, where figures, landscapes and moments will leave the visitor with a memory of a magical trip."

Jose Francisco Morales

Comisario de la Exposicion (Tenerife)

http://www.artesigloxxi.org

"I like to think that I am very versatile in my choice of subject matter," says Teresa. "My new surroundings provide the inspiration for me to paint on a daily basis and the fact that others may enjoy my work gives me the confidence to continue."

Website: www.artstopper.com